THE TENTH OF AV

The Do-It-Yourself
Jewish Adventure series

THE TENTH OF AV

KENNETH ROSEMAN

◆ ◆ ◆

UAHC Press
New York

Library of Congress Cataloging-in-Publication Data

Roseman, Kenneth.
  The tenth of Av.

  (The do-it-yourself Jewish adventure series)
  Summary: The reader travels back to the year 70 of
the Common Era to the city of Jerusalem, burning at
the hands of Roman soldiers, and must decide whether to
fight or flee—the first of many decisions throughout
the book—all concerned with real events in Jewish
history.
  1. Jews—History—Rebellion, 66-73—Juvenile fiction.
2. Plot-your-own stories. [1. Jews—History—Rebellion,
66-73—Fiction. 2. Plot-your-own stories] I. Title.
II. Series.
PZ7.R71863Te 1988   [Fic]   88-1343
ISBN 0-8074-0359-8

Maps by Helayne Friedland

Cover photo from The Granger Collection

FELDMAN LIBRARY

To Helen

whose constancy, despite all the changes
in our lives,
has been the best part of my life

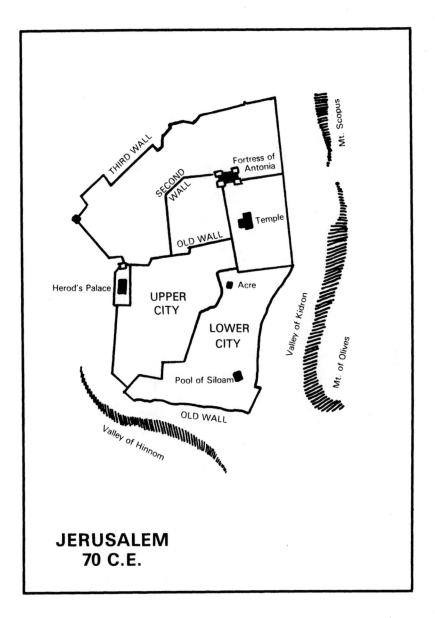

Mt. Scopus

Fortress of Antonia

THIRD WALL

SECOND WALL

OLD WALL

Temple

Herod's Palace

UPPER CITY

Acre

LOWER CITY

Valley of Kidron

Mt. of Olives

Pool of Siloam

OLD WALL

Valley of Hinnom

**JERUSALEM
70 C.E.**

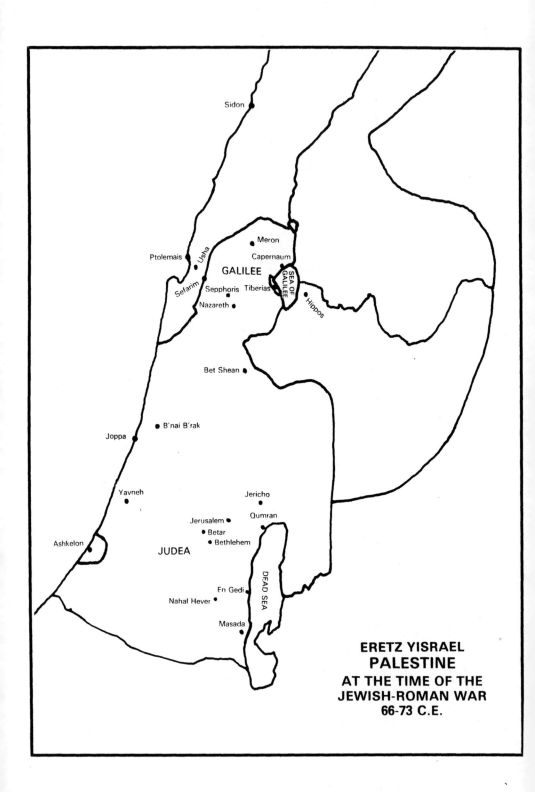

Sidon

Meron

Ptolemais

Capernaum

Usha

GALILEE

Sefarim

Sepphoris Tiberias

SEA OF GALILEE

Nazareth

Hippos

Bet Shean

B'nai B'rak

Joppa

Yavneh

Jericho

Jerusalem

Qumran

Betar

Ashkelon

Bethlehem

JUDEA

En Gedi

DEAD SEA

Nahal Hever

Masada

ERETZ YISRAEL
PALESTINE
AT THE TIME OF THE
JEWISH-ROMAN WAR
66-73 C.E.

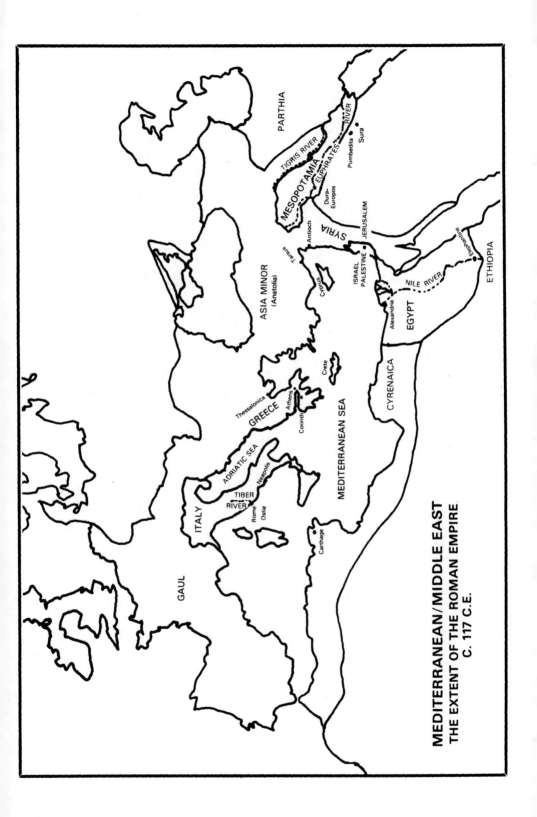

MEDITERRANEAN/MIDDLE EAST
THE EXTENT OF THE ROMAN EMPIRE
C. 117 C.E.

Hezekiah's water tunnel to the Pool of Siloam near Jerusalem.

The
Western
Wall.

The fortress at
Masada.

Ruins at Capernaum.

Dead Sea caves at Qumran.

THE TENTH
OF AV

The Second Temple in Jerusalem was destroyed by the conquering Romans on Av 10 in the year 70. Later tradition set back the date to Av 9 because the Talmud speaks of Av 9 as a day "disasters recurred again and again to the Jewish people." Thus, Av 9, Tishah Be'av, has come to be a day of mourning.

1

Do you know what history is? History is really very simple. History is about people, just like you, and the choices they make.

During their lifetimes, people are faced with various situations requiring them to make decisions. What choices they make and why is part of history. So is the way they react to the consequences of those decisions, which is to say, what they do next. History is the record of how real people in the past decided to do one thing or the other with their lives.

This is a history book. It contains lots of choices that you will make in your long journey back through time. This trip will take you back to the year 70 of the Common Era to the city of Jerusalem. To enjoy the many great adventures you will experience, you will need to use your imagination.

During the course of your historical journey, you will meet many people and face many problems. How the story turns out will depend on you, just as history depends on how other people in the past decided to shape their lives. Not all of these choices occurred in one person's lifetime; they have been changed a little so that you can work your way through a lot of different situations and experience what many people actually lived. In some cases, characters who lived a little before 70 C.E. or somewhat later have been brought into this story so you can get to know them. That's alright, however, because, in that sense, this book is historical fiction. But, please be assured, everything in the book actually happened to someone between the years 70–200 C.E.

2

An interesting question about choices is "Why did you select that and not this?" When you go to a store and make a purchase, you can ask that question. You can also ask that question of yourself when you make a crucial decision. Why did you choose what you chose? Most of the time, the answer is that one option appeared better than the other, more valuable. We call the reasons for such decisions "values," and you may want to think about the "whys" or the "values" as you read the book.

You may have already learned in your own life that even a very good choice may not turn out well. And, sometimes, if you get lucky, a bad choice can come out fine. At other times, there doesn't seem to be any way to choose between two alternatives. You just flip a coin and take whatever comes up. These possibilities also occurred in history, and you may want to think about them as you create your own historical adventures.

As you find words in italics, look them up in the glossary at the back of the book.

Now, turn to page 3 and get ready to move back through time. In the blink of an eye, you will be standing on the burning walls of the city of Jerusalem.

3

Red. All you can see is red . . . red flames against the early morning sky . . . red flames bursting from the roofs of the houses and shops near the Second Wall at the northwestern edge of Jerusalem . . . red blood on the bandages of the Jewish defenders of the city as the wounded drag themselves back from the fighting. Red. Everything seems a haze of dizzying red.

You turn to the tall man standing next to you and see something else. He is crying. Tears cascade down his face, and he makes no attempt to brush them away. Slowly, as if carrying a great weight on his back, he turns to you.

"My young friend," he says, "ever since your parents were killed, you have been my responsibility. Now, you are old enough to make your own decisions. Today, you will have to make the single most important decision of your life, whether to stay in Jerusalem and fight or leave the city with me. Let me try to explain the situation to you as clearly as I can."

4

"For four years, the Jews of the Galilee and Judea have been at war with the Romans. Some of us wanted only to be left alone as a Roman province, while others wanted to create an independent Jewish kingdom. The Romans, too, were divided. Some wanted only our taxes and peace in the region, while others wanted to destroy us, thus setting an example for those who would rebel against the Roman Empire.

"One thing led to another, and here we stand in Jerusalem, with legions of Roman soldiers surrounding our city. Josephus, our best general, has abandoned us to join the Romans. Yesterday, he stood outside our walls and pleaded for our surrender. But few people listened; most called him 'traitor.' Titus, the Roman general, has finally sent his troops into battle; now, the city has been set on fire. It is only a matter of a few days before Jerusalem is captured.

"Some people are ready to follow the revolutionaries and fight to the death. Their leader, John of Gischala, still holds out hope. He claims that Jews have defeated Romans before, and they will again. He thinks it would be better to die defending the holy city than be taken as a Roman slave.

"I disagree. My plan is to escape, try to make peace with the Romans, and keep Judaism alive. I'm not sure it is even possible to get out of the city, but I think it is worth trying."

You tell Yochanan ben Zakkai your decision.

If you choose to fight with John of Gischala and his forces, your Jewish pride preventing your backing down and surrendering, turn to page 5.

If you agree to escape with ben Zakkai, turn to page 6.

5

At first, there were other Jewish groups in Jerusalem who opposed the Romans. They also argued among themselves. On only one point could they agree: no surrender. Some rich and powerful Jews proposed a treaty of peace with the Romans, but the resistance fighters refused and killed the peacemakers; there was no more open talk of pacifying the Romans.

Gischala has a reputation as a courageous and successful commander. He is also very cunning and sly. Through trickery, he got the soldiers under Shimon bar Giora to enter the Temple during the Feast of Matzot in the year 69. They had left their weapons outside, but Gischala's men had not. Ambushed, bar Giora's soldiers were defeated and joined Gischala's army. Now, there was a single, stronger Jewish command.

Gischala knows that the Romans will attack on the northern side, through the weakest walls of the city. He stations his troops there, preparing for a major battle. You look over the wall and see the many thousands of soldiers in Titus's army. Suddenly, you understand. There can be no success, no hope. Yochanan ben Zakkai was right.

*If you decide to try to escape alone,
turn to page 7.*

*If you choose to hide, believing that escape
from a surrounded city is impossible,
turn to page 8.*

6

The Roman armies have completely encircled Jerusalem. At first, Titus and his generals even stood outside the walls and pleaded with the city's defenders to agree to a truce. Peace would then have been possible, but John of Gischala and his radical soldiers vehemently refused, actually murdering some of those who called for surrender. From that time on, compromise became impossible; war was unavoidable. With tear-filled eyes and bowed shoulders, you turn to Yochanan ben Zakkai. "It seems hopeless," you exclaim. "There's no way out. We are going to die."

"Nonsense!" he replies. "There is always hope. Let us think carefully." Suddenly, a smile crosses his face. "I think I have a plan."

A dreaded disease, possibly typhus, has been sweeping through the city. Thousands have already died from it. The Roman leaders are desperately afraid that it will pass beyond the city walls and infect their army; it could defeat them, even though the Jewish rabble could not.

Ben Zakkai has himself placed in a casket and asks you and five others of his students to carry him out of the city, as if he were a victim of typhus. The Romans step aside, allowing you to bear your dead teacher toward the cemetery. But, once out of their sight, you set the simple box on the ground, and ben Zakkai emerges, safe and healthy.

If you now decide to make your way through the devastated countryside toward the city of Yavneh,
turn to page 9.

If you choose to go north, where the war began but which has been peaceful recently,
turn to page 10.

7

How can you possibly escape from the city? Roman soldiers patrol all the walls; the gates are barricaded; at night, torches are lit so that anyone sneaking out will be seen.

You remember a story about a king, Hezekiah, who built a tunnel to the Pool of Siloam near Jerusalem so that water could be made available even if the city were besieged. Hezekiah lived long ago when the enemies were the Assyrians, but the tunnel still exists. You have heard people talking about it because that's the way they still get water.

You decide to explore the ancient tunnel. It might be a possible escape route, especially since it leads to the southern tip of the city, away from the main Roman forces. Maybe their patrols will be less careful there, and you will be able to slip through their lines. It's the best idea you can think of. What other choice do you have?

You grope through the slimy tunnel. Because a torch would attract attention, you must feel your way in the dark. Your feet are wet; your heart pounds with fear; rats scurry as you crawl through this narrow water pipe. Is there any exit?

About to give up, you see a light, faint at first, then stronger. There is a small opening. You climb through the hole, pause briefly, then run down the hill, away from Jerusalem. No soldiers have seen you. Your escape has been successful; you are now outside the southern end of the city.

If you decide to join a peaceful group of religious Jewish students who live at Qumran,
turn to page 32.

If you go to the Jewish fortress of Masada, still hopeful of defeating the Romans, turn to page 33.

8

Roman troops race through the city, setting fire to houses and stores, grabbing any merchandise they can steal, rounding up any people they can find. Your hiding place under a pile of torn clothing at the rear of a garbage dump helps you escape notice. Late at night, you sneak out to find some food. Just your luck! Some Roman soldiers have stopped at the edge of the dump to eat their bread and drink their wine. Quickly, they grab you and tie your hands together. Then, they lead you to the fenced-in field where Jewish captives are kept.

You see only women, children, and a few elderly people. "All the men were killed or taken away in chains," someone tells you. "It was awful. If the Romans found out, or even thought, that a man had tried to fight for Jerusalem, they executed him right away. Dozens of our husbands and fathers lie just over there, but we cannot even bury them properly. We mourn, but we are helpless to change the situation."

The next morning, the young people are divided into two groups. Chains are placed on your hands and feet; no escape will be possible. One group is marched toward the port of Ashkelon and put aboard a ship sailing toward Alexandria. The others are herded toward Ptolemais and placed on a ship which will land at the Roman port of Ostia.

*If you are on the ship sailing toward Alexandria,
turn to page 34.*

*If you are with the group landing at the Roman port of Ostia,
turn to page 35.*

9

The Romans approve of the peaceful policy of Yochanan ben Zakkai. "We had to destroy the city when Gischala insisted on defending it, but we much prefer to work with you. Continue your teaching; restore order and hope; help commerce and daily life return to normal. We shall not interfere with your religion, for you have been our friend."

An academy, established at Yavneh, elects ben Zakkai as its head. You continue your studies with him and are recognized as a very fine student. One afternoon, he invites you to sit with him and begins to discuss your future.

"My fine, young friend," he greets you. "Each of us has a job that God has appointed for us. Each of us must take part in helping Jewish life survive. You must now try to discover what it is that the Almighty wishes you to do. Some of us will be occupied with daily life, serving on the rabbinical *Bet Din* to decide immediate questions of Jewish life. Others will concern themselves with more academic and long-range considerations. Go! Pray! Ask yourself which path God has assigned to you and then follow it wisely."

If you choose to take part in the rabbinical court, deciding questions about food, shelter, business, and charity,
turn to page 36.

If you prefer to study such long-range questions of Jewish survival as what kind of leaders Jews should have and how best to pray,
turn to page 37.

10

The region just to the north of Jerusalem lies devastated. Even though the fighting was confined to the city itself, Roman soldiers have tramped through fields, taken animals for their food, and camped on farmland and in vineyards. The abundant destruction they have caused is obvious.

As you walk farther away from the burning city, however, there is less and less evidence of the war. By the time you reach Tiberias, a week's walk from Jerusalem, it is as though nothing had happened at all. The whitewashed buildings hug the shore of the lake, reflecting in its sapphire-blue water. Merchants hawk their wares in the streets while the sound of study and prayer can be heard through the windows of many schools. The area seems so normal you almost forget about the destruction and the immense changes that have just occurred.

When you think about the destruction of Jerusalem, however, you immediately understand that nothing can ever be the same as it once was. The cult of animal sacrifices is no more, and the priests have no function to perform. The center of Jewish life that was the Temple is gone forever. Everything is topsy-turvy. If Judaism is to survive, these leaders and institutions must be replaced by new ones. That is the job of the Jews who have escaped from Jerusalem.

If you and others in Tiberias decide to invite the great scholar, Gamaliel II, to lead you, turn to page 38.

If you believe you can make the necessary decisions by yourselves, turn to page 39.

11

A delegation from the Jewish community leadership meets with you. "Now that you have become very successful," they tell you, "we hope you will give something back to the community which ransomed you from Roman slavery many years ago and made it possible for you to have wealth and security."

While enjoying their praise, you wonder what they have in mind. Soon, their request is clear. They want you to become the collector of *tzedakah*, the official responsible for raising money to take care of needy Jews. Some of the money, you understand, will even be sent to the small Jewish community in Jerusalem so that there will always be Jews to pray at the Western Wall.

This is a request you cannot turn down. Your gratitude for what the Jews of Alexandria did for you when you were in trouble makes it impossible to turn your back on those who are now in need. "I accept. It will be an honor to participate in this *mitzvah,* in doing what God has commanded us to do." So, you begin your new career on behalf of the Jewish community.

If you decide to concentrate only on the collection of money,
turn to page 94.

If you choose to use your new occupation to lead you to deeper responsibilities and issues,
turn to page 95.

12

You take a job with a company that sells wine and oil throughout the eastern Mediterranean region. Because there are now Jews from Palestine scattered in many cities, you can do business with people who share your history and characteristics and whom you feel you can trust. Your trade prospers.

Much of the time, you must travel on ships, crisscrossing the sea, to supervise the buying and selling. To sail from Alexandria to Crete, Athens, Ostia, Carthage, and back may take most of a year, even with favorable winds and an experienced captain. While you are on such lengthy trips, you try to observe Jewish holy days and the *Shabbat.* It is difficult and, sometimes, you even lose track of which day is which. If clouds cover the moon at night, you cannot even be sure when a new month begins or when *Rosh Hashanah* occurs. You must find a way out of your confusion. There are *rabbis* who can help you in your dilemma.

If you decide to write to the rabbis who have gathered in the Valley of Rimmon in Palestine,
turn to page 58.

If you write to some rabbis in Jerusalem,
turn to page 59.

13

You exchange letters with leaders of groups in other Jewish communities. From Cyrenaica in North Africa to the island of Cyprus, throughout the Mediterranean area, Jews are secretly preparing for a rebellion against Rome. They are convinced—and you share their opinion—that problems elsewhere in the Roman Empire have weakened the ability of the rulers to oppose the planned uprising. While the Roman legions are busy in Parthia and Gaul, you and the other revolutionaries will rise up, overthrow the idols placed in the Temple at Jerusalem, and reestablish Jewish rule in the holy city. Now, you are certain, is the time to take up arms and fight for the restoration of Zion. You have no doubt about your success; you are sure you will enter the gates of Jerusalem in victory.

If you choose to participate fully in the proposed rebellion against Rome, turn to page 60.

If you decide to withdraw from the conspiracy, having reevaluated the conditions, turn to page 61.

14

You remember the teachings of Yochanan ben Zakkai, who showed you that violent revolt is not the way. People, you have come to believe, cannot restore the Temple; only the Messiah will be able to do that. "It is our job," you believe, "to follow God's commandments and to create a world of goodness into which the Messiah will come. Meanwhile, we must be patient."

These ideas influence what you will do with the rest of your life. You turn to the house of study and the house of prayer, spending most of your waking hours with the holy books. You study everything you can about how to live a holy and righteous life, and you are grateful for a Jewish community that makes it possible for you to live such a life without working.

You pray often, too, asking God to restore the rule of Jews over the Holy Land of *Eretz Yisrael,* to gather your scattered people back together in the shadow of the sacred Temple. You plead for a time of peace, justice, and joy; for a government led by a Jewish king, anointed directly by God or by God's prophet, Elijah, to serve as the messianic ruler.

One *Shabbat* morning, you hear a *haftarah* reading from the first chapter in the biblical Book of Ezekiel. Suddenly, you think that these words must contain the answer to your prayers. You share your ideas with a stranger sitting next to you, but he suggests another possibility.

If you are convinced that Ezekiel's words provide the answer you are seeking, turn to page 62.

If you decide that the stranger's alternative offers you a better chance to find your way, turn to page 63.

15

You wonder. Is it possible that what they are telling you really is true? They claim that the stories about Jesus fulfill predictions about the messiah made by ancient prophets. The great prophets of the Hebrew Bible predicted that God would become so angry with the sins of the Israelites that Jerusalem would be destroyed, and now that has happened. Maybe the Romans were, indeed, agents of God's displeasure. Maybe what has occurred really points to the end of the Jewish covenant and the beginning of a new relationship.

A friend who fled with you joins the group of persecuted Christians who are hiding in the catacombs of Rome. Every morning and evening, they hold services, drinking wine and breaking bread together to symbolize their commitment to their new savior. Neither you nor your friend reveals your choice in public. You do not want to be persecuted because you have remained a Jew; he is frightened because Christians are hunted down and killed by the Romans. Besides, he wants to earn money to send to the new churches as they spread the message of the new covenant.

You are not a member of this early Christian group, but you watch and listen with interest as they argue. Some believe that this new covenant is, in fact, a continuation and fulfillment of the ancient Israelite tradition. Others insist that Christianity is really different from Judaism, and there can never be a merger of the two.

If you believe that Christianity may be a continuation of Judaism, turn to page 78.

If you decide that the two traditions are totally different from each other, turn to page 79.

16

"**F**our of our great sages," you tell the group, "tried to enter Paradise. Each one met a different fate—some not so good, some better. You see, Jews believe there are many paths to heaven. If we respect each other and accept the idea that all people have the right to the religion they think is best, then we can live together in peace, as friends. People who think they have the only answer, the only truth, cause hatred and conflict."

The people who listen to you nod their heads and appear to agree. You hope that you have convinced them that the only way differing groups can live together in harmony is for each one to respect the choices of the others. "They may not be your choices," you remind them, "but, as long as they don't hurt anyone, people have the right to choose. Even if we think they are wrong, they still have that right."

If you have convinced your friends,
turn to page 80.

If you believe you have convinced your
friends, but you still have doubts,
turn to page 81.

17

You are satisfied that you have made the right decision. In the trading company where you work, you are promoted to assistant manager. You are married and have been blessed with two children. Other members of Rome's Jewish community respect you and often ask your opinion on important questions.

One evening, you and other leaders are called to the home of the president of the community. Two bearded *rabbis* sit at his table. You are introduced to them: Eleazar ben Azariah and Eliezer ben Hyrcanus. They are arguing so intensely that they hardly acknowledge your presence. But you listen in on their dispute.

They are talking about converting non-Jews to Judaism. Eleazar ben Azariah is urging that the doors remain wide open, that the Jewish community even encourage non-Jews to consider becoming Jewish. Eliezer ben Hyrcanus, on the other hand, is vehemently opposed. "They will only cause us trouble," he claims. "We have enough to do to help people who were born Jewish become good Jews. Who needs anyone else?"

If you are persuaded by the arguments of Eliezer ben Hyrcanus, turn to page 82.

If you prefer to side with Eleazar ben Azariah, turn to page 83.

18

"Why," your friends ask, "have you made the decision to abandon your comfortable life in Rome and return to the uncertainties of Jewish life in *Eretz Yisrael?* You must be crazy! Think very carefully, reconsider before it's too late."

But you have made up your mind. You have a special reason for wanting to return, a purpose that goes far beyond wanting to see the Holy Land again before you die. During your years in Rome, you have carefully observed many things around you. You know how Roman officials think, how their army functions, about the Christians who are beginning to collect in the city, about other religions throughout the empire. The *rabbis* who lead the Jewish community should know about your experiences and observations. They would be able to protect the Jews of the *Diaspora* more effectively if they really understood what the Romans were all about. That's why you must go back.

When you reach the Galilee, you explain your mission to the *rabbis*. Two of them urge you to join their academies to help them with their work.

*If you choose to work with Rabbi Meir,
turn to page 103.*

*If you prefer to work with Rabbi Akiba,
turn to page 104.*

19

Trying to separate the real poor from the fake poor is an almost impossible problem. You feel sad that some individuals take advantage of the situation to ruin it for everyone. However, there is no choice; the community must protect its small amount of *tzedakah* to use it for those who are really in need. It would be, some even argue, a sin against God to misuse money by giving it to people who do not deserve it.

The *Bet Din* suggests another way. It urges the community leaders to establish a central office where everyone who has need can come. That office can give money, food, clothing, and shelter to people according to their needs. It can also communicate with other towns in the vicinity. If they discover a fraud, the office can share its information with other towns. They, in turn, can share their findings.

The city leaders are delighted. Soon, *parnasim* are appointed to administer the *tamchui* and the *kuppah* and to collect money from others. "Even the poorest person should give some small amount," they decide, "because there is always someone even poorer."

The new system works well, but the city leaders are not sure what to do for *Pesach*, when new kinds of problems will arise. They must discuss this situation with the *Bet Din.*

Turn to page 66.

20

The *rabbis* cannot find a solution. On one hand, it is wrong to give money to someone who does not deserve it. That takes money away from those who really need it. But, on the other hand, if we prohibit begging, people who are desperately hungry will also be stopped from collecting, and that's also unfair. As one side presents its case, you think, "That's right!" But, as the other side argues, you say to yourself, "That's right, too!"

Finally, the *Bet Din* offers the city council its advice: "We cannot discover an easy way out of your problem. We think that it is probably better to allow a few fakes and frauds to collect money they don't deserve than to do something so drastic that really needy people would not be able to get the help they must have. Better to waste a few shekels than to leave someone without food or shelter. Continue doing what you have been doing all along."

"How wise they are," you think. "That's a decision that isn't really a decision. They are as wise as King Solomon!"

But the mayor isn't quite satisfied. "Learned scholars," he continues, "I understand what you are saying. But what are we to do for *Pesach* when there are special needs and problems."

Turn to page 66.

21

The *Bet Din* tells the city's leaders that they are allowed to prevent begging so that cheaters will not get the money that is meant for poor people. "Nonetheless," they continue, "you are not free to stop collecting and distributing *tzedakah*. You must find another way to help needy people. The Talmud teaches that all Jews are responsible for taking care of one another."

After the court session, you ask the mayor, "Have you ever considered opening a school where these people could learn a useful trade? If you would start such a school, soon they would no longer be poor, and we would have much less of a problem with *tzedakah*."

"What a genius!" the mayor screams out and immediately asks you to become the head of such a school. You had not exactly planned your life in this direction, but you can hardly refuse since it was your idea. You become principal of the new training school.

The *rabbis* of the academy at Yavneh urge you to offer a program where young students can learn to slaughter animals in the approved manner. "Our food must be strictly kosher," they insist, "and your students can learn how to make it so."

If you decide to teach students the occupation of slaughtering animals in the strictly kosher manner,
turn to page 67.

If you choose to teach students "regular" occupations,
turn to page 68.

22

When you return to the town of Yavneh, the first person you meet is Avdor, one of the most outstanding young scholars among those who have settled in this region. Many years before, a scholar named Shimon ben Shetach had begun working on a new document, the *ketubah* or marriage contract, which would be a protection for women when they marry. Particularly given the social chaos of present-day conditions, it is very important that each person's rights be carefully guarded.

"Avdor," you interrupt, "I know you are spending a lot of time working on your *ketubah* idea, but let me tell you what I have been thinking about. Schools! That's right, schools! We've got to build a network of schools so that Judaism will survive."

Avdor looks up from his parchments and smiles. "Funny you should mention that, my young friend. Just this morning, I told Yochanan ben Zakkai that we must demand that every community educate its children. Having a school must be a requirement in every Jewish town. That's how Judaism will be kept alive."

You break out in laughter. The two of you had thought of the same solution at the same time, and you are glad that the idea will be carried out. A number of scholars are appointed to open schools, and you are given your choice of which one to join as a teacher.

If you go with Yose ben Halafta to the town of Sepphoris,
turn to page 119.

If you stay with Eleazar ben Azariah in Yavneh,
turn to page 120.

23

"Fine," you think to yourself. "We know what the Torah is and who the prophets were. That's no problem. But there are lots of other books that could be in the Bible. Some are obvious, like Psalms and Proverbs, but others are not clearly in or out."

You turn to Yochanan ben Zakkai and suggest that he call a meeting of the leading scholars. "They could make a decision that everyone would accept. Besides," you remind him, "those Jews and Gentiles who consider Jesus as the messiah are doing the same thing. They are writing down their traditions and collecting them into what they consider a second volume of the Bible. We've got to be sure of what we consider holy books. Otherwise, there will be great confusion."

Yochanan agrees and summons the scholars and teachers. Together, you agree on almost everything. Only two books cause you trouble. Song of Songs and the Book of Esther pose problems because they do not mention God. They were obviously written rather recently and some passages in them are hard to think of as religious. Finally, you and the others figure out ways to include even these books.

There are some works which are excluded. Called the "Apocrypha," Hidden Books, they may contain good ideas or stirring stories like those of the Maccabees, but they just don't fit your idea of what belongs in the Bible. You feel content with your choices. All the arguments are settled; an agreement has been reached.

Turn to page 40.

24

The thought of becoming a *rabbi* excites you. If you become this new kind of Jewish leader, you can help shape the future of the people and its religion. Your influence would be immense, lasting for hundreds, maybe even thousands, of years. You realize that the decisions made in this time of catastrophe, disorganization, and chaos will have lasting effects for a very long time, and you enthusiastically approach Gamaliel II to ask him for rabbinical ordination.

He requires a great deal more study from you, and you apply yourself to the task of learning the Torah and the oral traditions of Judaism. It seems to take a long time, but the goal is in sight. You understand that you must prepare to be the very best *rabbi* possible. History will judge you harshly if you are not good enough.

Just before your ordination, however, a decree comes from Rome. The emperor Hadrian has forbidden any more rabbinical ordinations. Gamaliel, Akiba, and other great scholars travel to Rome to seek the repeal of this order, but to no avail. It appears that your future plans are blocked and frustrated.

*If you decide to join other students in
violating the ban and becoming a rabbi,
turn to page 69.*

*If you decide to continue to study and teach
the Torah in secret, despite the risks,
turn to page 70.*

25

The idea of becoming a *rabbi* frightens you because you really doubt that you have the learning necessary to be a truly effective leader and teacher. To accept such a responsibility is more than you are prepared to do at this time. Besides, you remember what Gamaliel's father, Shimon ben Gamaliel I, used to say: "Lo hamidrash ikar ela hama'aseh," study is not the central thing but action.

You determine that you will be a Jew of action. The quiet atmosphere of the academy does not attract you. Instead, you will be a builder of the community, a Jew who makes a difference in the daily lives of other people.

One idea you have is to help the children whose parents were killed in the Roman war. There are dozens, perhaps hundreds, of orphaned children in need of shelter, food, and education. Perhaps you should establish a school where they can live and grow up to be productive adults. Then again, being a schoolmaster may still be too quiet. Perhaps it would be better to live in a newly-founded village and work the land as a farmer.

If you choose to establish a school and become a schoolmaster, turn to page 71.

If you decide that life as a farmer would provide the action you seek, turn to page 72.

26

On *Shabbat* evening, you gather for a meal with your friends. Before you on the table are olive oil lamps, two loaves of bread, and a pitcher of wine. Everyone is joking; a lot of happy noise fills the room. Some of the people start to eat their dinner, but something troubles you.

"Wait a minute!" you cry out. "Wait! I know there's no more Temple, so we cannot usher in *Shabbat* the way our ancestors once did. But we could do something. Here, you light these oil lamps, just like the eternal light in the Temple." The strong flames of the lamps flicker across the room, casting shadows on the walls. Suddenly, the chattering noise ceases.

"Now, pour out some wine for everyone. Remember how we used to watch the priests perform a wine sacrifice? Well, each of us will be a priest. Raise your cups. Let's thank God for the good and sweet things of our lives."

Another of your friends leaps up and tears off a piece of bread. "Just like the loaves the priests blessed at the beginning of *Shabbat*." You are stunned by the special sense of holiness that enters the room. It is as if a queen had come in—a queen whose beauty and majesty are held in awe by everyone.

Turn to page 109.

27

Words, words, words—words are all you hear in the synagogue. There surely must be some better way to pray to God. One day, you take a long walk north from Tiberias. You pay little attention to the passage of time until you are surprised to find yourself in the small village of Capernaum. When you look around, you are in front of a synagogue. Perhaps, it would be better to call it a church, since Jesus prayed and supposedly did miracles here.

Some of Jesus' followers still live outside this building. They approach you and offer you wine and bread. Weary and hot from your walk, you sit with them and listen to what they say. "God does not want lawyers," they tell you. "All these commandments of what to do and what not to do— that's not what pleases God. What you must do is believe, have faith. Then, everything will be good in your life."

It's such a simple idea. You will be saved if you believe, not by your actions. You stay with these people. What they say is attractive, but it's almost too simple, too easy. You listen, but you're not persuaded.

It is hard for you, especially a Jewish scholar, to stay in this region. Some of the *rabbis,* like Joshua ben Hanina, are particularly angry at you and call you a traitor, for even listening to these new ideas. It would be safer to leave *Eretz Yisrael* and find a new home.

With sadness, but convinced that what you are doing is right, you begin your travels toward Rome.

Turn to page 64.

28

The caravan of donkeys and camels leaves Tiberias in the early morning. Most of the time, you walk alongside the animals, but occasionally one of the drivers lets you ride for a while. You travel for ten or twelve hours each day. Because the merchants want to sell their wares, which are loaded on the animals, as quickly as possible, it is important to reach the caravan's destination at the earliest date.

You marvel at the beauty of the mountains of Lebanon and Syria and at the growing power of the rivers as they rush down the green, forested hills. After about a six-week journey, you enter the Roman outpost of Dura-Europos. You help the merchants unload their goods and begin to sell them in the public marketplace. You raise your voice, crying out, "Fine leather for sale! Fine skins for sale! They're soft and warm. They'll make fine garments. Buy them while the price is right!"

You turn out to be a successful seller. Late in the day, the merchants turn to you and offer you a deal: "Stay here in Dura-Europos and be our representative, selling and buying. We shall pay you well. You can prosper here."

Lacking any other choice, you accept their proposition. You continue to succeed, and you do prosper. But something is lacking in your life. One day, as you are walking through a narrow, winding street, you are struck by the silence. You wonder why there are no sounds. Then, as you turn the corner, you hear a soft, rhythmic murmuring from one of the buildings, and you look in through the door.

Turn to page 73.

29

The ship on which you are sailing follows the southern trading route—from Ashkelon to Alexandria and then along the coastline of the Mediterranean—stopping now and then at towns to buy and sell. Finally, you arrive at the city of Carthage, far to the west of where you began.

You try to sell the goods that you have brought with you, but no one seems interested. In fact, you have the sense that the customers are actually avoiding you. If this continues, you will be unable to make a living; you may starve to death.

Toward nightfall, you approach another merchant who has been much more successful than you have been. "Excuse me," you stammer. "I cannot help but notice that you sold nearly all your merchandise while I couldn't make even one sale. What's your secret?"

"Don't you understand?" the storekeeper laughs. "You're obviously a Jew, and Carthage has become a Christian city. No one here will buy from a Jew. You can stand out there until it snows, but you won't have any success!"

Suddenly, all becomes clear to you. Now you must make a difficult choice. Either become a Christian or leave.

If you choose to convert to Christianity, turn to page 74.

If you decide to leave Carthage, turn to page 75.

30

The leader of this study group poses a problem: "In the days of the Temple, people brought their *Pesach* sacrifices to the priests in the Temple. Each group of worshipers presented a perfect lamb. Later, they roasted it outside the Temple and ate it during the night. Without a Temple, how can we now fulfill the *mitzvah* of offering a lamb to God at this season of the year?"

A hubbub of noise breaks out as everyone tries to suggest solutions. Finally, the leader regains control of the group. "Let the youngest member of the group speak first. That way, no one will be embarrassed by speaking against what a more senior member of the group has already said." He points to you. "You've just joined us. You speak first."

You stand up slowly, trying to collect your thoughts, and make a suggestion: "If people put a lamb bone on their tables during the *Pesach seder* and then read the words from the Torah about the sacrifice itself, would God find that an acceptable modern way to fulfill the *mitzvah?*"

More noise. Lots of talking and shouting. Everyone has an idea. Some like your suggestion; others are not so sure. Eventually, there is quiet, and the group turns toward the leader to hear his opinion. "I like it! It's worthy of Solomon. That's what we shall recommend to Rabbi Yehuda. Congratulations, our new friend. You have just made a major contribution to our work."

Turn to page 76.

31

The group to which you are assigned is debating what is required of a person who finds something that seems to have been lost. Some people think that the person who finds it must return it. After all, the Torah is pretty clear. It says that you should certainly return a lost object to its owner. But others are of the opinion that this isn't always true. "What happens," they object, "if there's no way for someone to prove that it was his thing in the first place? How will you know that you're returning it to the right person?"

Finally, you all agree on a simple procedure. "What the Torah must have meant," you decide, "is that the finder must try to return the object if two conditions can be met. First, the owner should be able to identify it and prove ownership. Second, the owner must still be hoping to have it returned. In that situation, the finder must make an honest attempt to return the found object. In other cases, it's finders keepers."

The group must now report its conclusion to Rabbi Yehuda.

Turn to page 76.

32

The Jews of Qumran receive you cordially. You bathe in the *mikveh* and dress in the rough, but warm, clothing they give you. A hundred or so men live in this community—quietly, peacefully—eating together, studying most of the day, copying holy books on parchment scrolls, praying. War, they tell you, is wrong. Soon God will restore the holy city of Jerusalem, and the Messiah will come. The right thing is to prepare: to be religiously pure and mentally ready. That is all a human being can do; God will take care of everything else.

You settle into the routine of the community, but something bothers you. Are you really ready, you ask yourself, to trust God so completely? Shouldn't people try actively to assist the divine plan? You are pretty sure that simply waiting is not the right way to go.

If you decide to take a more active role, even if it means fighting the Romans, turn to page 41.

If you choose to return to Jerusalem, believing that Jews should always be praying to the Holy One, even in a destroyed city, turn to page 42.

33

The hillsides east of Jerusalem are brown and dry with only occasional low, prickly bushes to break the monotonous view. Shepherds watch their goats and sheep and care little about you as you make your way along the paths. The days are hot, and you find it necessary to stop frequently to drink water from the leather flask slung from your shoulder; the nights are cool, and you sleep wrapped in your cloak, huddled against rocks or trees for protection.

At the ancient city of Jericho, you turn southward, along the coast of the Dead Sea. After walking several more days, you come to Masada, once one of the palaces of King Herod and now the refuge of nearly one thousand Jews who have fled from the Roman armies. The mountain rises abruptly from the plains; its sides drop off sharply. No one believes that any army could attack successfully up the steep cliffs. Supplies of water and grain are hauled up daily so that the defenders can withstand a very long siege.

As expected, the Roman legions arrive and establish camps both east and west of Masada. From above, they look small, but you know all too well how powerful these soldiers are. Having seen them in action, you realize that there is probably little hope for your survival.

If you choose to stay at Masada, having come too far to surrender now,
turn to page 43.

If you decide, having second thoughts about your situation, that giving up is the wisest course of action,
turn to page 44.

34

When you land at Alexandria, you are marched, actually dragged, through the burial ground to immense grain warehouses. Having heard the stories from the Torah, you are reminded of similar structures at *Pithom and Raamses*, built by the Israelite slaves in the days of Moses. Are you condemned to repeat the ancient history of your people?

Suddenly, there is great commotion at the Gate of the Necropolis (cemetery). A delegation from the very large and wealthy Jewish community of Alexandria has arrived and is meeting with the Roman commander. You overhear, "It is a duty of our religion to ransom our fellow Jews if they are captured." Though you cannot hear every word, you can see that agreement is reached; a large sum of money passes to the Romans; then, you and the others are released, unharmed, overjoyed once again to be with Jewish people.

You stroll about two miles across the city to the Jewish quarter. From that area, you can look over the New Port and see all the way to the Tower of Pharos, guarding the busy harbor. You are then accepted in the home of a Jewish family, where you bathe and are fed. The next morning, you join the others in prayer. After worship, you must make a decision about your future. The leaders of the community advise you to enter into business. They are sure that you will never return to the Holy Land. But you are not sure you can accept this idea.

If you go into business in Egypt,
turn to page 45.

If you can't accept living outside Israel,
turn to page 46.

35

The trip to Rome takes over a month, your ship crisscrossing the Mediterranean. You see the devastation of Jewish communities, as the Romans have brutally suppressed the rebellion and put thousands of Jews to death. Other Jews, pitiful captives, are marched as slaves before your eyes, but there is nothing you can do to help them. At least, not at this time.

When you enter Rome, you are amazed. It is even grander than Alexandria, although you had never believed that any city could be. Nestled among seven hills, the city centers around the Forum, with the huge Colosseum at one end and a brand new archway being built at the other. You decide to investigate this new construction.

When you arrive at the building site, you are told that it is a monument to celebrate Titus and his capture of Jerusalem. Then, you notice that Jewish slaves are being forced to build this structure which testifies to their own defeat and humiliation. Within the arch itself is a carving of the menorah being carried away from the Temple. You resolve, right then and there, that you will never walk under this arch. The Romans may shame you, but you will never willingly humiliate yourself.

Noise from another side of the Forum attracts your attention, and you turn in curiosity to find out what is happening. A parade of some sort is entering the public area.

Turn to page 47.

36

Three famous *rabbis* form the *Bet Din*. You have not yet been ordained, but you assist the *rabbis* by copying down the arguments of the people who appear before the court and the decisions that the learned scholars make. You listen carefully and learn a great deal.

One day, members of the city council of Yavneh come to seek an opinion from the rabbinical court. "We have a problem," the mayor begins. "You, of course, know that the fighting has left many people without food and shelter. We know that it is our responsibility as Jews to care for such unfortunate people, even if they are strangers. After all, having read the Torah, we know that we must be especially thoughtful of the stranger who comes to us for help. But we also know that some of the people who come for help are not really needy. They go from town to town, begging, asking for *tzedakah*, taking money that ought to be used for really poor people. Since it is hard to tell the really needy from the fakes, we are considering prohibiting begging in Yavneh. What do you think we should do?"

If you believe the rabbinical court should advise the city council to issue a decree against public begging but find another method to organize tsedakah distribution, turn to page 19.

If you feel there is no way to solve the problem and the council must continue as before, turn to page 20.

If you feel the council should prohibit begging but find an alternative to help the poor, turn to page 21.

37

You walk away from Yavneh to sit quietly and think about your future. Many changes have occurred in Jewish life within the last few years. The Temple is gone and with it the cult of sacrifices and the jobs of the priests. Now, you wonder, how will we communicate with God? Who will lead us? Now that the Temple is destroyed, where will the center of our life be? Now that Jews are spread throughout a very large region, how will we keep Judaism intact and unified? Is it possible that there will eventually be many different Judaisms as the distant communities each go their own way?

You think about the conditions of life in *Eretz Yisrael.* The Roman war has left disorganization and chaos, and you realize that strong leadership will be needed if those questions are to be answered in such a way as to guarantee the survival of Judaism. Above all, it seems that now is the time that some difficult decisions need to be made. You and the others at Yavneh will need to advise Jews throughout the world about the right thing to do, how to behave, how to pray, what to study, what is holy and what is not. This is a heavy responsibility, but you see no alternative. Without such steps, Judaism will disintegrate.

If you decide that the secret of survival is in building schools,
turn to page 22.

If you believe that survival depends on the choice of books to be in the Bible,
turn to page 23.

38

Few other leaders have the reputation for combined brilliant scholarship and gentle and thoughtful personality as has Gamaliel II. When he arrives in Tiberias, you sense that a very special man has come into your city. He is very wealthy, to be sure, but his legal rulings have always considered the welfare of poor people. His servant, Tabi, tells everyone how kind he is. You learn that some of his decisions are particularly concerned with the rights of women. You also learn that his humility will extend even after his death, for he has expressly forbidden people to bury him in anything but the most ordinary way, dressed in a simple linen shroud. This seems to be a leader who can help reestablish Jewish life.

Gamaliel informs you that there are really two major crises. One is that of leadership. Without the priests, who will lead the people? Some of the students will need to concentrate on filling this vacuum. Others, he says, should try to help reorganize the forms of worship. How people will pray to God, now that the Temple and its cult are gone, is a most important problem. Much depends on the way this is worked out. Each student in Gamaliel's academy must select one of these two problems to study and recommend solutions.

If you choose to work on the issue of leadership,
turn to page 48.

If you decide to help the Jewish people find new ways to pray,
turn to page 49.

39

"**W**ho needs outside scholars to tell us what to do? We can rebuild our lives all by ourselves. We've read the books of the Torah many times. Surely, the answers are all in those holy words."

But it doesn't turn out to be so easy. Everyone in town has a different idea. The Torah talks about the Temple, but now there is no more Temple. As you argue and discuss, nobody has a solution about what should be done. It seems that you have reached a dead end.

One of your friends is convinced that the only thing to do is wait—wait for a word from God—wait to die—wait for something.

On the other hand, you think that perhaps you were wrong about not seeking the advice of a scholar. Maybe you should travel to Sepphoris and consult Rabbi Yehuda Ha-Nasi. He is supposed to be a very wise and thoughtful man. He might know what to do.

If you decide to wait, praying to God for an answer to your questions,
turn to page 50.

If you choose to go to Sepphoris to consult Yehuda Ha-Nasi for advice,
turn to page 51.

40

One day, as you enter the house of study, you cannot believe your eyes and ears. You thought that all the difficulties had been settled, but here are Akiba and Ishmael ben Elisha screaming at each other. Had not their friends stepped between them, they would have come to blows.

Akiba is shaking a fistful of writings. "Every word in the Torah means something. God would not have put anything in the Torah without a purpose. Even a little word, like "et," must have a meaning. If we study the Torah carefully enough, we can figure out God's intention."

Ishmael groans sadly. "My respected colleague, don't you see what you are doing. If you can interpret 'et,' which really has no meaning at all, then you can interpret anything. You will be able to find any idea you want in the Torah. I am convinced that the Torah speaks in the language of people so that we can understand it. Let us read it as though God were speaking to us, without artificial interpretation, without strained meaning. There is enough in the Torah without forcing it to say what it does not mean. Common sense is what we need."

With each of them struggling in the grip of their supporters, you leave the room. "Which of them is right?" you wonder.

If you decide that Akiba is probably right, turn to page 52.

If you choose Ishmael's way of reading the Torah as the better way, turn to page 53.

41

If Jews are ever to live with dignity and self-respect in their own country, they must fight for what they believe. You've come to share this idea, and you realize that just sitting in Qumran among a community of religious students won't accomplish your goal. You cannot wait for God; you must take action.

Your decision makes you feel good. To be strong and to stand up for your beliefs give you a sense of power and energy. A *rabbi* in the Galilee named Akiba ben Yosef has been preaching resistance to Rome. You travel to hear him speak. He reads from a scroll which he calls the "Apocalypse of Baruch," a message that the Messiah will come very soon, that the Temple will be rebuilt, and that the Judean state will be restored to all its former glory. If this is true, you think, you've chosen the right path.

Akiba advises you to join Shimon bar Koziba at En Gedi. "He may even," Akiba whispers to you, "be the Messiah."

If you accept Akiba's advice,
turn to page 54.

If you decide to stay in the Galilee, sparing
yourself a repeat of the horrible scenes of the
bloody terror of the battles in Jerusalem,
turn to page 55.

42

When you reenter the city of Jerusalem, you can hardly find the places you once knew well. Debris from fallen buildings lies in the streets; packs of dogs scavenge for food; and large areas of the city are totally deserted.

Near the Temple Mount, the destruction is even more obvious. A foot-thick layer of ashes and rubble lie all around the holy area, evidence of the Roman policy to destroy the glorious Temple. You trip over a pointed stone, noticing the inscription, "lashofar," for the shofar blower. It lies upside down, thrown a hundred feet down off the walls. No shofar blower will ever again stand on this stone to proclaim the new year, the new moon, or other special days.

The sacred Temple no longer exists. There remains standing only a small section of the outer, western wall, a section that is not even part of the Temple itself. You and others huddle there, begging every day for food and praying that a Jewish army will return to Jerusalem, rebuild the Temple, and bring a national restoration.

One day, you hear rumors of a new military uprising under Shimon bar Koziba. He claims to be the messiah, and such learned scholars as Akiba agree. Perhaps just such a man will restore the Temple and bring God's presence and Jewish rule back to Jerusalem.

If you fear the Romans will crush a rebellion, ending all hope for a Jewish return to Jerusalem,
turn to page 56.

If you choose to leave the city to find bar Koziba's supporters,
turn to page 57.

43

Once you make your decision to stay, you feel wonderfully happy. Finally, you will face the Romans directly and fight for what you believe. No more running and hiding. Your choice of resistance gives you strength; your friends remark that even your walk seems springy and excited.

The Romans have built a long ramp up the western cliff of Masada. Day after day, you and the other defenders notice that the top of this artificial slope reaches closer to the summit, and you realize that it will be only a short time until hundreds of Roman soldiers will be able to walk onto the top of the mountain. There is plenty of food and water. In fact, you pour buckets of water over the side of the hill to show the Romans that they will not be able to force you to surrender because of hunger or thirst.

But you will die. That is clear. Eleazar ben Yair, the commander of the defenders, calls everyone together in the synagogue that overlooks the Roman ramp. "My friends," he says, "it is better that we take our own lives and those of our families than be killed or captured by the Romans. *Kiddush Hashem,* dying in loyalty to God and the Jewish faith, is a special privilege. We must perform that *mitzvah.*"

Later that morning, five of you gather and draw lots. One will kill the other four, then commit suicide. The last thing you feel is the sharp edge of a knife on your throat. *"Shema Yisrael,"* you speak, and it is over.

END

44

During the night, you slip away from the Jewish defenders and make your way down the steep and winding path on the eastern side of the mountain. The descent is dangerous in the dark, but it is the only way you have of escaping certain death. When you reach the bottom, you surrender to the Roman guards.

They put you to work building a ramp on the western side of Masada. For twelve hours each day, you and other Jewish captives carry rocks and wicker baskets of earth up the ramp, and you realize that it will soon be high enough for the Romans to reach the summit and overwhelm the defenders. "How can I do this?" you think to yourself. "Those are my friends on Masada, but I am contributing to their deaths." You have no choice. Should you refuse to work, the Romans will kill you instantly.

When rumors of the death of Eleazar ben Yair and the Jewish defenders and their families reach you, you sag against the wall of the Roman camp and cry. "How could I have left my friends? I should have been there to die with them. I am a traitor, guilty; I have sinned."

The Romans march you away from Masada to the seaport of Ashkelon. You are herded onto a sailing vessel and taken to begin a new life, captive in the great city of Alexandria.

Turn to page 34.

45

Every morning, you recite the words of the Psalmist, "If I forget you, O Jerusalem..." But repeating words and changing history are two very different things. You have come to accept the reality that the holy city lies in ruins. Occasional Jewish travelers bring reports that only a few Jews actually live in the city and that even the sacred Temple grounds have now been turned into an altar to the Roman emperor. You know there is nothing you can do to reverse these events, and, sadly, you turn to make a new life for yourself.

You have found a job in a trading business. Ships arrive in the port, bearing large clay jugs of wine and oil. Your workers unload them and place them on carts. Then, they pull the carts to stores and warehouses, where you sell the products. With the money you receive, you purchase vegetables, dates, and other agricultural products which you send to Rome and to Greece on the same ships.

In time, you become rather wealthy. God has blessed you with money and family, and you are happy. As you grow older, however, you wonder if this is the right way to spend the rest of your years.

If you decide to retire and devote your time to the work of the Jewish community, turn to page 11.

If you choose to continue in business, feeling that this is your best contribution, turn to page 12.

46

Alexandria is one of the greatest cities in the world. Here you are, and you should feel the excited pulse of its life, the hustle and bustle of its commerce, the strength of its population, and the wonder of its schools and libraries. Yet, you do not. Instead, you feel sad and downhearted.

Alexandria may be a wonderful city; it may even possess a growing and active Jewish community. But it is not Jerusalem. It cannot compare to the Holy Land where the presence of the God of Israel can be felt with every breath. Your sins and those of your people must have been very great, indeed, for God to have punished you with *galut,* with exile from the Holy Land.

You feel incomplete. You know you can never feel fully Jewish until you return to *Eretz Yisrael.* Somehow, you must go back, regardless of the cost, regardless of how difficult life will be for you once you resume living in the shadow of the destroyed Temple. There are even some Jews in the *Diaspora* who still believe that Jerusalem can be reconquered with an army.

If you decide to join the Jews who believe in the reconquest of Jerusalem by force, turn to page 13.

If you choose to try to find a peaceful way to return to Zion, turn to page 14.

47

To your great dismay, you observe a river of dejected, shabby, filthy, chained men and women being driven forward by Roman soldiers. There can be no doubt. These are the prisoners taken from Jerusalem, taken from various Jewish communities which had revolted against Rome. At the head of the column are the leaders. When all the captives are assembled in the Forum, surrounded by soldiers and jeering Romans, the leaders are led forward, one by one, and executed. Their bodies are left unattended, a warning to anyone else who would defy Roman power. The others are then marched off for lives of slave labor, pain, and sorrow. Such, you see, is the fate of those who rebel against Rome.

Several dignified Romans now step forward. You can tell by the gold jewelry and rich cloth of their togas that they are important and powerful. "Come with us," they almost command the crowd. "Let us go to the temple of the emperor and offer sacrifices to him, the god-ruler who has made this glorious day of victory possible."

"Is it true," you wonder to yourself, "that the Romans consider their human emperor to be a god? It must be. Why else offer sacrifices to him?" Suddenly, you feel frightened. You cannot possibly participate in this cult of idolatry; God would surely strike you dead, a Jew who betrayed the Holy One of Israel. You must get away before you are swept up in the crowd of worshipers.

If you choose to run toward the underground catacombs, a well-known hiding place, turn to page 64.

If you decide to try to find the Jewish community of Rome, turn to page 65.

48

To you, it is clear that leadership is critical. Without leaders, the people will be lost. That's the one issue you must help solve.

The priesthood was hereditary. If you had been born into a priestly family, you would have been a priest. There was no other way to become one. The priests' learning was limited to the performance of Temple sacrifices and matters connected with religious rituals; other areas of Jewish life simply did not concern them. It's pretty obvious that a totally new kind of leader will be necessary under the emergency conditions of *Eretz Yisrael.* You turn to your fellow students and exclaim, "We cannot turn away any qualified people. Whoever has the skills and learning to be a strong leader is needed to restore order and give us a sense of direction. We've got to find another way besides the traditional priests."

They agree—but what to do. You think and study together for a long time. One *Shabbat,* while the Torah is being translated from Hebrew into Aramaic, your ear picks up something unusual. The person translating is adding his own comments. You jump up. "Wait a minute! That's the answer! We must have learned teachers who can interpret the Torah for new circumstances and conditions. What we need to look for are people who can teach, regardless of what family they come from. What we need are *rabbis.*"

*If you decide to seek ordination to become
this new kind of leader,
turn to page 24.*

*If you choose to seek another career,
turn to page 25.*

49

You once heard an old man who had returned from a trip to Rome say that worship there was like going to the theater. The dramatic presentation captured the attention of the assembled congregation; they felt emotionally attached to what the priests were doing. Now that you think about it, the rituals of the priests in the Temple in Jerusalem were also pretty dramatic. They lifted up the animals to be sacrificed, killed them, and placed the bodies on the fire before God's altar. Meanwhile, Levites in colorful robes paraded around the sanctuary, chanting psalms, and spreading sweet-smelling incense. You remember watching people as they walked out of the Temple. What they had seen moved them; they felt that they had really been in the presence of the Almighty God, that they had participated in something important.

Now, of course, all that is gone. But the people still need that feeling of being in touch with God, of sensing something holy and special, of doing acts which go beyond everyday life. That's what you and the others must find, rituals that will replace those of the Temple. Not an easy task! "How," you wonder, "can we offer thanks and praise to God and pray for help? We must find some new ways. But how?"

If you believe that the solution lies in the new synagogues of the Galilee, turn to page 26.

If you are convinced that a more radical answer is needed, turn to page 27.

50

Dejected, terribly sad, you sit quietly in a corner, your shoulders bowed as if you were mourning a dear friend's death. "With no Temple, there can be no hope." That's what your friends have decided, and you are forced to agree.

Still, it is painful. To stay in the Holy Land and watch the slow death of God's chosen people is an agony you can hardly bear. In fact, it's an anguish you will not allow yourself to suffer. You will force yourself to leave, to go somewhere else. At least then you will not have to watch the end of the Jewish people.

There is a caravan of merchants leaving for cities in Mesopotamia. You can join them and travel toward the east. Your other option is to go by sea as far as you can across the Mediterranean. Miles of sea between you and *Eretz Yisrael* might drown out the sorrow that is breaking your heart.

If you choose to join the caravan,
turn to page 28.

If you decide to leave by crossing the
Mediterranean,
turn to page 29.

51

Rabbi Yehuda greets you warmly and welcomes you to join the students and scholars of his academy. When you share your concern with him, he puts his arm around your shoulder, reassures you, and begins to relate a story.

"Long ago, near Athens, there lived a Greek innkeeper named Procrustes. When travelers came to spend the night, he offered them a bed. But he had a bed of only one size. If someone was too short, he would stretch out the guest; if someone was too tall, he would cut off enough until the guest was short enough for the bed.

"If the Torah were like that, we would, indeed, be in deep trouble, for we do not now fit the exact words of the Torah. Fortunately, however, the Holy One revealed the solution to Moses. When Moses came down from Sinai, he carried two Torahs: the written one you know and an oral one. The oral one helps us adjust the written one to new situations. God's law is for all times, but it must be applied to changing circumstances. That is what we try to do in this academy."

Rabbi Yehuda tells you that there are two groups working on such problems. One group is studying new ways to celebrate *Pesach.* The other group is dealing with everyday problems. He suggests that you may want to help.

If you choose to help the group studying Pesach,
turn to page 30.

If you decide to work with the group dealing with everyday problems,
turn to page 31.

52

In his academy at B'nai B'rak, Akiba ben Yosef expounds the verses in Deuteronomy 5:12–15 which contain the fourth of the Ten Commandments. "Shamor et yom hashabbat lekadesho," he recites, "observe the Sabbath day and keep it holy. You notice," he continues, "that the 'et' has no translation. Yet the perfect God has included it in the commandment. It teaches us something. What is that lesson? Some say that it means that we ought to pray and study throughout this entire day. Others interpret it to mean that it is this very day and only this day that can ever be the Sabbath."

Over to the side of the room, a disciple of Ishmael ben Elisha throws up his hands in disgust. "That's the most ridiculous thing I've ever heard. How do you know, Akiba, which of these interpretations or hundreds of others might be the correct one?"

Akiba turns angrily toward the young scholar and tells him that Elijah the Tishebite, the prophet who announces the coming of the Messiah, will solve the riddle. *"Teyku,"* he says, "Elijah will decide. Meanwhile, if you are unhappy with my teaching, go over and study with Ishmael. If you want to be misguided and misled, he can help you."

Akiba's sarcasm annoys you. Maybe Ishmael has a better understanding of this verse.

If you decide to accompany the young scholar to the other academy, turn to page 53.

If you're still not satisfied, after reading page 53, turn to page 77.

53

Ishmael ben Elisha sits, smiling, at the front of the class. When he speaks, everyone leans forward to hear each word. Today, he is discussing the two versions of the Ten Commandments, especially the fourth one about the Sabbath day. "You will notice," he begins, "that the Exodus 20:8 version starts with 'zachor,' remember, whereas the Deuteronomy 5:12 commandment begins with 'shamor,' observe. Now, there are some scholars who think that this means something very hard to understand. But they are wrong." You know he's referring to his rival, Akiba, but he's too polite to mention him by name. "God is simply teaching us two very clear lessons. Exodus uses a negative approach, of not working on the *Shabbat.* Deuteronomy takes a more positive attitude, telling us the things we are supposed to do on this special day, like saying blessings over candles and wine and being joyous."

It all makes good sense to you, but not to everyone in the class. One of the students stands up and objects. "But what about the word 'et.' You have not translated it. God surely must have put it in this commandment for a purpose. What does it mean?"

Ishmael laughs. "I really don't know. Perhaps when Elijah the Tishebite comes to tell us of the approach of the Messiah, he will also solve this puzzle. Meanwhile, Akiba likes to worry about little words like that. Why don't you go over to his academy and ask him?"

If you choose to walk from Yavneh to B'nai B'rak where Akiba teaches, turn to page 52.

If you're still not satisfied, after reading page 52, turn to page 77.

54

En Gedi is a beautiful oasis on the western shore of the Dead Sea. Tall palm trees bear plentiful crops of dates, while graceful willows grow beside springs of water. Harvests of spices, especially balsam, and fragrant *etrogim* fill the air with pleasant odors. It's hard to believe that this is also the headquarters of the man who is preparing to challenge the Roman armies of what is now called Palestina.

You are put to work, minting coins. The *sela'im* that you stamp bear palm trees or grapes on one side and, on the other, the inscription, "Shimon: Year I of the Freedom of Jerusalem." Just to read those words gives you hope, and you shiver with excitement.

But, as the Roman armies advance against bar Koziba, whose name has now been changed to bar Kochba, "son of a star," to indicate that he is really the Messiah, you must make a decision.

If you choose to join Shimon as he heads toward Betar to fight the Romans, turn to page 86.

If you decide to hide out with many of the residents of En Gedi by climbing into nearby caves, turn to page 87.

55

Staying in the Galilee was a wise choice. You hear daily of the fighting south of Jerusalem, and each report is more grim than the one before it. The army of Shimon bar Koziba has been besieged at Betar; it will certainly be defeated, and the entire force will be massacred. In mourning, you cut your robe as David did when he learned of the death of his son Absalom and sit on the ground for seven days.

Following the disaster, the Romans pass very strict laws. No one may be ordained as a *rabbi*. It is a crime to teach the Torah; it is illegal to study the sacred Law. Some Jews counsel patience and predict that these restrictions will soon pass. You are not so sure. You are certain, however, that you can no longer accept compromise with the Romans, and, though you cannot resist with military force any longer, you must find a way to fight back.

Rabbi Shimon bar Yochai and his son have decided to leave the town of Meron and go into hiding in a nearby cave. Friends will supply them with food and water, while they continue to study Torah. You ask permission to join them, and they agree.

Turn to page 88.

56

Your judgment was correct. Shimon bar Koziba's forces are defeated within three years; mercilessly, the Romans punish or kill anyone associated with his rebellion. Jews are now forbidden to live within the city walls of Jerusalem.

Christians, however, had nothing to do with the uprising; they carefully stayed away from anti-Roman activities. As a result, they are not forbidden to live in the city. Having been taught that the worship of Yahweh must never depart from this holy city, you now see only one way to prevent that unthinkable possibility.

You convert to Christianity, but, privately, you continue to observe Jewish rituals. Since Jesus lived a Jewish life, what you are doing cannot be all wrong. Meanwhile, you pray at the Western Wall, as close to the ruins of the Temple as you can approach, hoping that God will send the Messiah to restore the fortunes of your people.

Your double identity is never discovered. You spend the rest of your life in prayer and study. Toward the end of your life, you wonder if God has heard your pleas. No messiah has come. Perhaps you have chosen the wrong path. But, there is always hope. Maybe tomorrow you will be able to practice openly the Jewish rituals you must now practice secretly. Maybe tomorrow . . . maybe . . .

END

57

Y ou travel northward from Jerusalem through Sepphoris and then to the little town of Meron, just to the northwest of the Sea of Galilee. As you sit on the rocky hillside, a man approaches, surrounded by about twenty students. "Who is this man?" you ask. At once, everyone wants to tell you about Joshua ben Hananiah: how Rabbi Joshua prevailed when he went to Rome to argue with the emperor Hadrian who ordered that the Temple never be rebuilt; how welcoming and generous he has been to converts to Judaism; how he follows his own advice that the right path through life is to acquire good friends. Everyone seems to love Rabbi Joshua.

You listen intently to his teaching. "War is wrong. My own *rabbi,* Yochanan ben Zakkai, taught this lesson, and I agree. We shall never bring the Messiah with military might. God respects only good deeds, prayer, and study. That is what we must stress. Those who resort to armies will only bring disaster and calamity."

What Joshua ben Hananiah teaches makes sense to you, but not to everyone. Others are persuaded by the arguments of Rabbi Akiba who believes that Shimon bar Koziba is the Messiah or, at least, that he will bring the Messiah when he defeats the Romans with his troops. Advocates of both points of view urge you to join them.

*If you choose a more active, military solution
to restore Jewish rule over Palestine,
turn to page 84.*

*If you are convinced that a more peaceful
approach is the path to take,
turn to page 85.*

58

It takes nearly an entire year, but you are overjoyed when a messenger comes to your door in Alexandria with a letter. He has carried it on a caravan across the Sinai desert, making very sure it was safely delivered. You give him a purse of coins as a reward for having been so careful.

The letter comes from three of the most important *rabbis* of *Eretz Yisrael,* the land of Israel, as you have begun to call it. Rabban Shimon ben Gamaliel II now serves as the chief rabbi and is, therefore, addressed as rabban, not simply *rabbi.* Assisting him are Rabbi Meir and Rabbi Yose ben Halafta, and your letter is signed by all of them. They explain that they have formed a *Bet Din* since your question is a very serious one, a question that is asked by many of the Jews who were exiled from the Holy Land.

"If Judaism is to survive," they begin, "we must be prepared to make changes. Of course, one cannot alter the calendar, but we must make it possible for Jews all over the world to observe the holy days correctly. Therefore, we decree that a second day be added to certain holy days: *Rosh Hashanah* and the three pilgrimage festivals of *Pesach, Shavuot,* and *Sukot.* That way, even if there is confusion, Jews outside *Eretz Yisrael* will be able to keep the holy days properly, without mistake. May God's special blessing rest upon you."

Turn to page 89.

59

*R*abbis in Jerusalem! There are no *rabbis* in Jerusalem. You have forgotten that very few Jews are even allowed to live in the holy city. The Roman governor of Syria-Palestina permits Jewish worshipers to approach the Western Wall only on the Ninth of Av, the day of mourning for the destroyed Temple. By allowing them to enter only on a day of defeat and exile, the Romans accomplish their purpose: to humiliate and embarrass Jews everywhere, reminding everyone that opposition to Rome ends in disaster.

With no response to your letter, you become depressed. Without a festival calendar to unify Jews throughout the world, Judaism will soon be observed differently in different lands, and, after that, will disappear. Without a common religious practice, you know that Judaism cannot survive. Saddened and in despair, you have no hope for the future of your religion.

But you cannot live without hope. Desperately, you investigate other sources for the future.

If you believe that some of the Egyptian religions will fulfill your needs, turn to page 90.

If you explore different thoughts about a hopeful Jewish future, turn to page 91.

60

The revolt begins in Cyrenaica in the year 115 and spreads during the next two years to many Jewish communities on the eastern Mediterranean coast. The emperor Trajan had sent his best military forces far to the east, hoping to conquer Parthia and annex it to his empire. You are convinced that the absence of these legions will make it possible for your rebellion to succeed.

However, you have underestimated the power and the determination of the Roman ruler. He calls for reinforcements, bringing troops from other places in the empire. He also appoints a new commander, Quintus Marcius Turbo, and gives him a simple order: "Put down the uprising at any cost. Punish the ringleaders. Make sure the Jews understand that they cannot succeed and that they must never attempt such a foolhardy rebellion again."

Marcius Turbo suppresses the revolt against Rome cruelly and viciously. You hide, moving stealthily from house to house during the night. But you cannot escape the knowledge that you have failed and that most of your friends and allies have died painful and agonized deaths by crucifixion, the typical Roman method of executing traitors and rebels. You were obviously mistaken in supporting the rebellion. Now, it is clear that, if you want to live, you must flee from Alexandria.

If you decide to travel up the valley of the Nile River,
turn to page 92.

If you prefer to sneak aboard a ship and try to find refuge in Antioch,
turn to page 93.

61

The uprising against Rome begins. Many Jews are excited and hopeful, but you have second thoughts. You have witnessed the strength of the Roman army, and you suspect that the conspirators have underestimated the determination of the empire to crush any revolt. When the Jewish rebels come to your door, you decline to participate. They argue, then leave, angrily yelling curses over their shoulders. You are convinced you have made the right decision, but you are sad that your former friends cannot see the wisdom of your point of view.

And wise it was, indeed. Within barely days, the rebellion is crushed and its leaders executed. Rome's power was never more obvious; clearly, it was not God's will that the uprising succeed.

You now come to a second conclusion. The Alexandrian Jewish community had been the center of the revolt. The Romans will never let that community become strong again; Jewish life in your city is over, its glory now only a matter of past history.

You think. If Rome is so strong, perhaps you ought to live at the center of that power. There is an active Jewish community in Rome, and you know some of the people who live there. Packing your few possessions, you pay for passage on a ship that will sail to Ostia, the port near Rome. As the harbor lights of Alexandria sink below the horizon, you wonder what the future will bring for you.

Turn to page 35.

62

The words of Ezekiel echo in your head: Carried aloft on a chariot of fire . . . escorted by creatures that were somewhat human, but with wings, with faces of animals, spouting flames . . . a vision of the heavenly court and God's own throne . . . and the voice of the Almighty. Such an image surely contains within it the answer to all your prayers if only you could understand it correctly.

You begin to devote more and more time to the study of the secrets of this heavenly chariot; it soon occupies all your attention. You neglect your family and friends, your job, your physical appearance, even your health. Those who care for you try to persuade you to stop this constant preoccupation with Ezekiel, but you have become convinced that what happened to him will happen to you. You are now sure that God will send such a chariot and escort to carry you back to Jerusalem.

As days, then months, then years pass and the dream has not been fulfilled, you continue waiting. But the frustration has its effect and gradually you become deranged, completely detached from the real world.

You end your days, sitting on the bench in the synagogue in Alexandria, praying for the time when God will take you up to heaven—waiting patiently, praying, waiting, hoping —praying.

E N D

63

After services, the stranger introduces himself to you. He is Rabbi Joshua ben Hananiah, and he is returning to Yavneh after a mission to Rome. He has tried to persuade the emperor Hadrian to allow the Jews to rebuild the Temple in Jerusalem. "It might just be possible. The emperor didn't say no." He pleads with you to return with him to Yavneh. "A great day is coming. We shall soon be able to live a full Jewish life in *Eretz Yisrael* again. You are the kind of young person we need with us. War and violence are not the answer; they will never bring the kingdom of God to earth. But the study of Torah will; that is the only way. You must come with me."

You consider his offer and his urging very carefully. For years, you have hoped to set foot again on holy soil. Now, the opportunity has been offered to you. How can you refuse?

When Joshua ben Hananiah leaves Alexandria, you go with him. The words of Psalm 122 suddenly become real to you: "I rejoiced when they said to me, 'We are going to the house of the Lord.' Our feet stood inside your gates, O Jerusalem, Jerusalem built up. . . ." As you travel the final miles with Rabbi Joshua, your smile widens; you are, indeed, very glad.

Turn to page 9.

64

You wind your way through narrow streets, trying not to attract any attention to yourself. The catacombs are ancient burial grounds, shunned by many Romans, which is why some unpopular people find them good hiding places. When you reach the area, you pause, then plunge into one of the openings in the ground.

It is dark inside, and you feel your way along the underground corridor, groping on the slimy, damp walls. In one niche in the wall, your hand comes to rest on an unfamiliar object, but then you recoil—human bones. You continue on.

As you turn one corner, you see a light at the end of the tunnel, and you move toward it quickly. Seated around a small fire is a group of families.

They introduce themselves as Christians, a sect persecuted by the Romans even more than the Jews. The Romans are afraid that the Christians will be disloyal to the Roman Empire, and they do everything possible to make life difficult for them.

You listen respectfully to their worship service and hear them talk about Jesus, whom they believe to be the messiah or Christ. "Since Jesus came to earth," they explain to you, "there has been a new covenant. The old covenant of the Jews has been replaced by a new one of the Christians. We hope you will consider fulfilling the promises of your Bible by joining our group."

If you decide to spend some time with the Christian group to hear their ideas, turn to page 15.

If you respond with a story from Jewish tradition, turn to page 16.

65

You wander through the streets of this great city, looking for any familiar sight, anything that would lead you to the Jewish community. The Roman government considers Judaism a "religio licita," a legitimate religion, but, since the revolt of Bar Kochba, it has become unpopular and even dangerous to be Jewish publicly. As a consequence, it is hard to find where Jews live and do business.

As you turn a corner near the Tiber River, however, well-known sounds strike your ears: the Hebrew language—the sound of children rehearsing their lessons. You enter the building and discover a small synagogue. The teacher greets you. Soon you have found a new group of friends, a job as a clerk in a trading company, and a place to live.

One *Shabbat* morning, a guest speaker ascends the pulpit and addresses the congregation. He is a *shaliach,* a messenger from *Eretz Yisrael,* sent to raise money for the Jews still living near Jerusalem and to urge others to return to the Holy Land. You listen carefully to his words. They call to mind distant memories, and your eyes become moist. It was special to have lived in the most holy place in the world. It would be nice to go back.

If you choose to remain in Rome, your new city, even after careful consideration, turn to page 17.

If you decide to follow the shaliach and begin your return trip or aliyah, turn to page 18.

66

The problem of *Pesach* has come up only in the last few years. When the Temple stood in Jerusalem, a community such as Yavneh would send a delegation to the Temple. The delegation would present an unblemished lamb to the priest who would sacrifice it. Then, they would eat the roasted lamb outside the Temple during that night, together with *matzah* and bitter herbs, and they would retell the story of the Exodus from Egypt.

Now, because the Temple has been destroyed, Passover must be celebrated at home. The rabbis have begun to describe an orderly ceremony around the table, telling the Exodus story; drinking wine; and eating *matzah,* bitter herbs, greens, and other foods. Because the meal has a special arrangement, people have begun to call it a *seder.*

But, what about the poor? They must also be able to celebrate this holiday, as all Jews are commanded in the Torah. The *Bet Din* tells the mayor and city council that they must make provisions so that every Jew can fulfil the obligation of drinking four cups of wine and celebrating the *seder* meal. As soon as you hear this, you know what you will do with the rest of your life; you will concentrate on helping all Jews celebrate *Pesach.*

If you decide to travel throughout the Diaspora, collecting money and sending it to Eretz Yisrael so that Jews there can continue to observe the Passover, turn to page 114.

If you remain in Yavneh to collect Passover money and food for the poor, turn to page 115.

67

Ever since the Temple was destroyed, the *rabbis* have been issuing new regulations about food. You know, of course, that the first twenty-three verses of the eleventh chapter in the biblical Book of Leviticus contain a long list of foods which you may and may not eat. But the *rabbis* have gone further, erecting what they call "a fence around the Torah." Some of them tell you, "It used to be that you could assume the purity of Judaism because it was mostly under the control of the priests in Jerusalem, and they could be counted on. But now, the Jewish religion is primarily practiced at people's homes. According to the Talmud, the dining-room table has replaced the sacrificial altar of the Temple. We must help people keep Judaism pure by informing them of the right thing to do. Students in your school can be immensely helpful by learning how to prepare meat in the approved fashion."

Following their advice, you train students in the art of "shechitah," ritual slaughter. But you are not entirely satisfied. There must be more to life than just being a religious official.

One beautiful summer afternoon, you gather together all the students of the school and tell them that you are going on a trip.

Turn to page 116.

68

You really do not want to teach young people only to be religious officials. There are only a limited number of jobs of this sort, and not everyone is suited to them. There must be more for young students to learn. In addition, those who earn money from "regular" occupations are the ones who will be able to support the work of the *rabbis,* the academies, and the activities of the Jewish community. "We need people besides *rabbis* and scholars," you decide. Therefore, the new school you open concentrates on teaching students more ordinary skills. That way, they will be able to earn a living and also contribute *tzedakah* from the money they make.

But you cannot teach everything. You and the city council members discuss what occupations will become the specialties of the school. Some have one opinion; others differ. You are unsure about whose advice to take.

If you decide to teach agricultural skills,
turn to page 117.

If you prefer what you call the "M and M
Solution,"
turn to page 118.

69

Roman soldiers march through the countryside, entering towns, ransacking schools, doing everything possible to disrupt Jewish life and study. Wherever they find a school, they destroy it and much of the town around it. Innocent people are punished along with those who violated Roman orders by studying the Torah. The persecution under Hadrian is fierce and painful.

You leave Tiberias with a few other students and meet Rabbi Yehuda ben Bava between the cities of Usha and Sefarim. He agrees to ordain all of you in an open field so that the Romans cannot take vengeance on the inhabitants of the nearby cities since they did not shelter the illegal activity.

As he places his hands on your head and pronounces the blessing, Roman legionnaires come around the bend in the road. "Run!" he counsels you. "I'll delay them."

You and the other new *rabbis* dash in the other direction. Looking back, you witness a horrible sight: the body of Rabbi Yehuda with a dozen Roman spears embedded in it. He has given his life for *Kiddush Hashem*, as a martyr in praise of God. Bitter tears cascade down your cheeks as you turn to continue your flight.

If you decide to hide and continue teaching in the Galilee,
turn to page 105.

If you choose to leave the area, suspecting that Jewish life will not be possible here for a long time,
turn to page 106.

70

What Hadrian orders is evil and wrong. In the past, whenever Rome had conquered another people, the Romans had always been willing to leave the religion and culture alone. Their subjects had only to pay taxes, keep the peace, and provide workers for building roads and other public structures. Now, Hadrian is changing the rules; he wants everyone to be like the Romans, worship the emperor, and abandon their previous rituals.

You cannot do that. God was revealed to Moses at Mount Sinai. When Moses came down the mountain, he transmitted the Torah to the Jewish people who agreed to obey it and live by it. That ancient promise still binds you; you are not free to violate it. You certainly cannot stop teaching the Torah, the book of the rules of the covenant.

Together with other *rabbis,* who feel as you do, you hide out in the Galilee. During the day, Roman soldiers search for you, without much success. A few teachers are caught; they are tortured and die a horrible death. Because the people are on your side and send the Romans in the wrong direction, most of you are not caught. At night, you slip into the towns and hold classes in the back rooms of people's homes.

One night, as you are secretly instructing the class about the laws of holiness, you hear a knock on the door.

If the Romans have finally caught you,
turn to page 107.

If you are about to get a different message,
turn to page 108.

71

It certainly doesn't bother you that you are not going to be as famous as some of your friends who have chosen to be *rabbis.* Their legal opinions are quoted widely, and people often journey long distances to attend their lectures and classes. That's no problem for you. "I would have made a terrible *rabbi,*" you often say. "I am glad I chose to be more energetic and active."

Active you certainly are. You collect as many orphaned children as you can find. While the teachers of your new school help them learn to read and write, to follow the *mitzvot,* and to engage in occupations, you travel through the countryside, asking people to contribute for the support of your school. To farmers, you say: "Some of these children are learning how to work metal. They will make new tools for you. Please give us some food for them to eat." To townspeople, you plead: "We are teaching the children how to add and subtract. Soon, they will be good clerks for your stores. Please give us money to buy clothing and food for them."

When you return to the school after a long day's travel, you are exhausted. Most of the time, you are successful, and the school seems firmly established. But, every night, before you fall asleep, you read a chapter from the Torah. Rabbi Ishmael had taught you long ago that the ideal life is a combination of Torah study and worldly occupation, and you are convinced he was right. In fact, your life is really about as right as any life could ever be; you are indeed a very happy person.

END

72

With some other friends, you establish a new village between the Sea of Galilee and Hippos. There you dig huge holes in the ground. The work is backbreaking as you shovel load after load of dirt out of the long, deep pits. When you have finished each hole, others open a gate at its end and flood it with water from the sea.

Soon your village looks like houses surrounded by ponds of shimmering, reflecting water. But under the surface a miracle is happening: in each pond you have put thousands of tiny fish that will soon be large enough to harvest. When that happens, you will be able to provide food for many people. That will be a significant *mitzvah*.

You recognize that scholars and *rabbis* are necessary, but, for you, active work is even more important. You enjoy getting the dirt of the Holy Land under your fingernails, and you thank God for the opportunity to work the land and feel the satisfaction of producing needed food. Besides, you often tell your friends, "If we were all *rabbis,* who would be able to live? Where would we find food? If we have to depend on others for the basic necessities of life, we shall never be a normal people. Some Jews must be farmers, blacksmiths, fishermen, cart drivers; we must be prepared to do every kind of work. That is the only way a Jewish society can work properly."

You end your days with a sweaty forehead and calloused hands—but with a full and thankful heart.

END

73

There are many people seated on rough wooden benches, swaying and chanting together. You have met some of them in the marketplace, but you have never had a personal conversation with any of them.

You look around as you enter through a small, arched doorway. On the walls there are paintings. As you examine them, you recognize some of the subjects: Abraham and Isaac at Mount Moriah, Moses at Sinai, David slaying Goliath, Solomon building the Temple—all of them are scenes from the Bible.

Then, listening to the words more carefully, you are astonished. Hebrew! They are praying in Hebrew! Tears come to your eyes, and you sag against the wall. You can hardly believe it. Here, in a distant outpost of the Roman Empire, you have stumbled upon a synagogue of Jews. As you realize more fully what has happened, you begin to smile. You have found a home. Dura-Europos is no longer a foreign place. With friends and a synagogue, you can live a life of Jewish meaning and value, even here.

E N D

74

You think a long time. Your ancestors stayed Jewish throughout many difficult times. Would you be a traitor if you left the faith now? Without a Temple, is Judaism finished anyway? Perhaps the decision was made for you when the Roman legions burned the city of Jerusalem and destroyed God's holy dwelling place. If there can be no Jewish future, why not go ahead and become a Christian? There's certainly no point in staying Jewish.

You turn toward the church, asking the leader of the congregation for help. He arranges your baptism, and you officially join a new community. As soon as you take this step, your commercial fortunes change for the better. People come to your stall in the square to buy what you have to sell. You do not become wealthy, but you live nicely, marry, and have six fine children.

There's only one problem in your life. Everytime you go to the docks to buy new merchandise from arriving ships, you meet Jewish merchants. You overhear them talking about synagogues and *rabbis,* about prayers and *tzedakah,* and many other things you remember from your childhood. "Is it possible," you think to yourself, "that Judaism has survived? Could I have made the wrong decision?"

You'll never know. Too much of your life is now connected to the Christian community of Carthage. Although you know you would be welcomed back to Judaism, you decide you can never turn back to live your life another way. As you grow old, you must live with doubt, for you have no other choice.

END

75

Boarding a ship at Carthage, you journey across the Mediterranean to the port city of Neapolis. Almost as soon as you step onto the shore, you see men with covered heads, and, as you listen, you hear them exchanging private words in Hebrew and Aramaic. There can be no doubt; these are Jews like yourself.

You stop one of them and introduce yourself. He greets you warmly and offers you a place to stay until you find a room of your own. "Taking in travelers has been a *mitzvah* since the days of Abraham."

You are overjoyed at this cordial welcome and decide immediately to remain in Neapolis. It is a busy commercial and trading city with ample opportunity for success. Eventually you do, indeed, succeed in business, and you and your family become important leaders in the city's Jewish community.

You know that you can never return to *Eretz Yisrael,* but you still miss the Holy Land. To make up for the loss, you take upon yourself a special obligation. Whenever Jews from the land of Israel come to Neapolis, you offer hospitality and send them back with a generous contribution of money to support those Jews who have remained in Israel. Your gifts will help them continue their studies and prayers. You are sure that these acts of *tzedakah* will make it easier for Judaism to survive. That makes your life seem worthwhile.

END

76

When you and the group leader tell Rabbi Yehuda about the new idea, he is pleased. However, you keep asking more questions. Whenever Rabbi Yehuda gives you an answer, you seem to find a dozen more questions.

Finally, Rabbi Yehuda tires of giving answers. "Enough questions! Stop asking new ones everytime I answer." When you ask why, he gets annoyed and chases you from the room.

Still, he understands that you are not different from many other Jews. You want to know what it is that God wants you to do, how to fulfill the Torah's commandments, how to know what the right thing is, and how to do it. Questions—questions—questions. But Rabbi Yehuda Ha-Nasi finally answers the questions.

Turn to page 124.

77

"*T*eyku," you mock. "Neither one of them knows what he's talking about. All they can do is wait for Elijah. There must be another teacher who has the answers."

And so there is. Or, at least, there seems to be. Eliezer ben Hyrcanus holds his classes in an olive grove outside town. As you sit in the back row of students, he tells you about a question of whether or not a particular stove was usable. "The sages said it was unfit, but I disagreed. You should have seen the miracles I performed. A carob tree moved fifty yards down the road; a river ran backwards; a building's walls leaned in but did not fall; even the voice of God was heard, siding with me."

"But, honored teacher, what happened in the argument? Did you win?"

"No! Would you believe that, in spite of those miracles, they voted against me. It must have been a plot they had worked out in advance. They always want to be the ones to decide the law. Even if God tells them the answer, they vote for whatever they planned to decide in advance. It's just not fair."

You agree that Eliezer has a point, but it is clear that Akiba and Ishmael are always going to be more important than he will ever be. You decide to return to one of their schools.

If you decide to go back to Akiba at B'nai B'rak,
turn to page 110.

If you prefer the school of Ishmael at Yavneh,
turn to page 111.

78

Being Jewish has always been important to you, and you would never abandon your faith. But here, you have discovered, there are people who combine Judaism with Jesus, a way of fulfilling the promises of salvation made in the Bible. They can keep the dietary laws, pray in Hebrew, wear a talit, and, in fact, maintain all the religious practices you were taught as a child. The Gospel of Matthew even quotes Jesus as saying that not the slightest bit of the law will ever be changed, that he came not to overturn the law but to fulfill it. Yet, they can also believe in Jesus, called Christ in Greek and *mashiach* in Hebrew.

There are members of the group who say that "Christianity is really the second part of Judaism. Let's keep it that way. Don't spoil it by borrowing practices from other religions." Others in the group oppose this. They want to attract non-Jews to the faith. They think that it is not a good idea to talk so much about law and duties. They favor bringing in pagan members, even if it means being less Jewish in the new church.

If you agree with those who reject adding rituals from the Roman "mystery religions," turn to page 96.

If you decide to listen in on those who wish to combine parts of many religions, turn to page 97.

79

Now, the choice is as clear to them as it is to you. Either Jesus of Nazareth is the messiah, the Christ, or he is not. There cannot be any compromise, and they must choose Christianity or Judaism. One cannot be both Christian and Jewish at the same time.

When they reread the letters of Paul, they come to the conclusion that this man who contributed greatly to the development of Christianity was sure of two things. First, this Jew from Tarsus, who changed his name from Saul to Paul, was convinced that Jesus was the messiah. Second, he learned quickly that most Jews would never accept that belief. He taught that Christianity would be spread most widely among the pagans, non-Jews who lived along the shores of the Mediterranean.

Paul traveled widely, spreading the good news. This mission is called "evangelism," and it is to this task that your friends commit themselves. Nothing, they conclude, would be more important than bringing the message of salvation and eternal life to people who have not yet heard it.

Their major concern is where to preach in order to win converts to the new faith. They could go to the Greek cities of Corinth and Thessalonica. On the other hand, they can travel even further east to Antioch.

If they go to Corinth and Thessalonica, turn to page 98.

If Antioch is their choice, turn to page 99.

80

The Christians of Rome agree with what you teach. "Surely," they say, "we do differ with the Jews. They think that one can be saved by doing good works, by what they call *mitzvot,* whereas we believe that salvation can only come through believing in Jesus as the Christ. There's no way to compromise. But the Jews have the right to live the way they want, and we shall not try to interfere with it. After all, Jews must also be part of God's eternal plan."

Their response makes you extremely happy. You feel that your preaching in the marketplaces of Rome and in its churches has succeeded. Now, it is time for you to turn to a more stable and settled occupation.

You open a small hotel, a hostel in which travelers can find hospitality, a warm meal, and a comfortable bed. Every evening, people from many different cities gather at your table, exchanging stories and news. You share your religion with them, especially stories from the Bible and tales of the early *rabbis.* You may no longer be preaching in public, but you are still preaching the message of salvation. You have found a task that gives your life great meaning. You devote the rest of your days to sharing the good news with those who come to your inn.

E N D

81

"**Y**es, that sounds right. We agree. Each person may believe whatever seems best. Of course, you know that we would never try to force our beliefs on anyone else."

Their words bring comfort to your ears. You turn away with a smile because you are convinced that you have taken a major step in healing the wounds that separate Jews from Christians. Harmony and friendship are a certainty in the future.

As soon as you walk away from the group, however, they turn to each other with different words. "What kind of foolishness is this? Many truths? Each person has the right to differ? Nonsense! We know that we have the truth and the only right beliefs. It is our duty to share them with others, to bring everyone into our community. Did not Saint John teach that no one can approach God except through God's son, through Jesus?"

Little do they realize that you had not gone so far that you could not overhear their whispers. You are astounded. What they said to your face is contradicted by these new expressions. Suddenly, you understand that, with these people, there can be no room for tolerance, no respect for someone who has another point of view. You cannot live among people whose way of looking at the world is so narrow that they cannot accept other people for what they are.

You cannot remain with the Christians. The only solution is to return to Judaism. You gather your belongings and walk out of the house. Down the street, you turn a corner and head for the synagogue.

Turn to page 65.

82

At first, your tendency was to offer hospitality and welcome to anyone who wanted to become Jewish. "Why shouldn't we make converts?" you said to your friends. "Are we ashamed of being Jewish? Isn't our religion the one that God revealed to Moses on Mount Sinai? We should share it with anyone who wants to learn about it."

But then you had a change of mind. Sitting behind the desk of your store, you overheard a conversation between a convert and a Roman official. The convert was telling him about plans in the Jewish community to support a rebellion against Rome. You realized that the convert was a spy. This led you, perhaps unjustly, to suspect all converts.

You become known as an outspoken opponent of conversion. "Converts," you claim, "delay the coming of the Messiah. We must set boundaries. We cannot let everyone and anyone into our community. Let us be Jews, and let them be anything else they want. We don't want them, and we don't need them!"

Turn to page 100.

83

"**W**ait a minute!" you think to yourself. "Here in Rome every other group seeks converts to its religion. No one is shy about trying to persuade others about the truth of what they believe. Why should we be any different? After all, isn't Judaism a beautiful religion and a good and ethical way of life?"

You walk down the street, more and more convinced that Eleazar ben Azariah was right. You must be prepared to teach non-Jews about Judaism and to welcome them into your community if they choose to become Jewish.

At the end of the street, you pause. There is a fork in the road, and you must decide which way to turn. One road would take you into the center of Rome, to the Forum with all its activity, its people, its noise, and its excitement. The other road leads back to the Jewish community.

If you decide to take the road to the Forum, turn to page 101.

If you choose the road back to the Jewish community, turn to page 102.

84

The army of Shimon bar Koziba has established its headquarters at the oasis of En Gedi on the western shore of the Dead Sea. In this beautiful city of palms and balsam trees, you find a hustle bustle of activity. Armorers forge weapons; merchants trade all sorts of goods; scribes sit at the feet of learned men, copying down their words on strips of papyrus and leather—everyone prepares for the triumphant return of God's presence to Jerusalem.

As you walk through the streets of En Gedi, you become convinced. There can be no other way; Rome will never surrender voluntarily; if Jews want to control their own land, rule their own future, they will have to expel the Romans by force. "Jews," you think to yourself, "have been weak too long. We study and we pray, but now is the time for action. Why would God help us if we won't have courage and help ourselves?"

You join the forces of Shimon bar Koziba and volunteer for whatever work will help his cause.

Turn to page 54.

85

You've seen the Roman soldiers camped near Jerusalem. You've seen the devastation of the holy city. You know that a ragtag band of Jewish recruits has no chance to defeat this powerful army. Rabbi Joshua is right; fighting will lead to destruction. You elect to stay as far from the revolt of bar Koziba as possible.

And you are right. His first attack, on *Sukot* in the year 132, seemed successful, but soon the Roman might asserted itself, and the rebels fell back. Within three years, they are besieged at the fortress of Betar and captured. Everyone who has joined them is either killed or captured and sent into a life of Roman slavery. Many of them, you suspect, would envy the choice you made, but it is too late to change their fate. All you can do is continue on your path.

You enroll as a student in the academy of Rabbi Meir in the north of Israel. With his students, this gentle and wise man collects Jewish teachings. "One day," he predicts, "some scholar will organize all that we have done. It will be a special book, a book which will help Jews wherever they live remember how to live a good and pious Jewish life. That time is not yet upon us; now, all we can do is gather the sayings and decisions of wise leaders. We shall help Judaism survive."

You share his goal and his conviction that Judaism will live when Jews study, pray, and practice charity. To make that happen becomes your life purpose. You are content; you have chosen a wise and satisfying path.

END

86

At the fortress of Betar, only about fifteen miles southwest of Jerusalem, Shimon bar Koziba (bar Kochba) has gathered a large and well-armed military force. You feel good that you are among those who will defeat the Roman legions and return Jerusalem to the glory of its past. Shimon tells you that you are taking an active role in God's plan, and you believe him.

A Roman general named Sextus Julius Severus has other ideas. With a huge army, he moves south from Jerusalem and encircles Betar. You discover that you are completely cut off, and there is no escape. Slowly, but surely, Sextus tightens the circle, while your supplies of food and water diminish. The hope that you had at the outset is now gone; instead, calamity and disaster appear certain.

Finally, the legions of Sextus attack. The hungry, thirsty, weakened Jewish troops mount what resistance they can, but in vain. This time, there will be no survivors; the Romans will make sure that your reward for resistance is the sword or the spear. The three years of bar Kochba's freedom of Jerusalem are over, and so too is your life.

E N D

87

You and the other refugees pack carefully. Only the most important things can be taken with you: keys to the storehouses of En Gedi to which you eventually hope to return, precious glassware for *Shabbat,* legal documents written on papyrus in both Hebrew and Aramaic and then wrapped in leather, and your special tunics with stripes and ritual wool fringes sewn on each corner.

In a dry river valley called Nahal Hever, west of En Gedi, you climb up a steep cliff and enter a large cave. There you will be safe from the floods which race down the hillsides in the spring. It is unlikely that the Romans will be able to find you.

Unfortunately, a Roman patrol makes its camp at the top of the cliff above your hiding place, and the smoke from your fires attracts attention. Sitting in your cave, you can hear the noise of the patrol, and you know that the enemy is upon you. Realizing that the Romans will not let you escape, you bury all your precious goods and prepare for a lingering death from starvation and thirst. The revolt is over; there is no way out.

END

88

What you did not expect is that you, Rabbi Shimon bar Yochai, and his son, Eleazar, would be in that cave for twelve years. You learn a lot of Torah, a very great deal indeed, but you are glad when the Romans finally lift the restrictions and the three of you can emerge from your concealment.

Rabbi Shimon asks you to accompany him on a mission to Rome. "There are other restrictions," he tells you, "which make it impossible for Jews to study and practice as they should. We must plead with the emperor and the Roman Senate to ease these rules so that we can act as God wants us to. The Messiah cannot come until Jews are free to study and perform *mitzvot* in the Holy Land. The Torah makes this very clear." Naturally, you agree to travel with him.

The trip to Rome is a great success. The emperor assures you of freedom to fulfill your duties as Jews, except in the city of Jerusalem, now called Aelia Capitolina. As a penalty for Jewish rebellion, Jews are banned from the city. Still, you return to a life of Torah and *mitzvot,* certain that your choices have been correct and that you have contributed to the survival of Judaism for future generations.

END

89

What a wonderful idea! A second day of holy days for those who live so far from the land of Israel that they may make an error and, unintentionally, commit a sin. The more you think about it, the more sense it makes.

As you continue your business career, traveling back and forth across the seas, you now have another mission and a purpose: to share this information with every Jewish community to which you come. To the leaders of the communities, you explain that this will make it possible for Jews all over the world to observe *Shabbat* and all the festivals without error. This is another means by which all Jews will be unified because they will all be praying the same prayers, blowing the shofar, lighting the candles, gathering for *seder* at the same time, no matter where they live.

You remember the third verse from the second chapter in Isaiah, "For out of Zion shall go forth the law and the word of the Lord from Jerusalem." Now, you understand how correct that ancient verse is! Teachers from *Eretz Yisrael* have properly interpreted the calendar; the word of God has come from the Holy Land; now you must spread the message to the four corners of the Jewish world.

Not every Jewish community you visit accepts the new idea, but you persist. As you grow old, you realize that your mission is slowly succeeding. Change takes time, but you feel that you have had a small role in helping Judaism survive under new conditions.

END

90

Egyptian neighbors invite you to accompany them to the Temple of Isis. Isis has the power, they tell you, to conquer death. After all, she raised her husband, Osiris, from the dead, and she can give life and an eternal future to anyone who is a member of the religion.

Having nowhere else to turn, you begin to learn the mysteries of the cult of Isis. After a lengthy period of studying the secrets of the faith, you spend an entire day fasting and then are initiated as a member. Since very few who begin the study are actually accepted, you feel proud and special as you pull on the distinctive shirt which marks true believers.

Every week, you gather with other members of the Isis cult for a ritual meal. The priest hands you food, telling you that this is really the body of Isis and consuming it will give you eternal life. "The unity of our secret brotherhood and the triumph over death! That is what we offer," he exclaims.

You question whether this strange religion really works. Can anyone actually live eternally? Of course, you understand that you cannot satisfy your doubts until you yourself die—and you would rather wait. It's easier to live with questions than to die for answers. But, the hope you now feel through simple, unquestioning faith in Isis is better than the doubts you had about Judaism and the Jewish future. That is the path you choose.

E N D

91

You feel alone, abandoned. The Jewish God seems so distant and unapproachable. Yet, you want desperately to believe in some power, some force which will be close to you, which can offer you comfort and support, which you can love, to which you can even talk. The God of the Torah and the prophets doesn't respond to these needs. You are about to look elsewhere for a religion.

As you walk down the street slowly, your back bowed and your eyes downcast in worry, you pass a Jewish school. You hear the voices of children through the windows, and you pause to listen. One youngster is reading the eighteenth verse of Psalm 145 from the Bible: "God is near to all who call upon God, to all who call upon God in truth." It is as if God had answered your prayers, right there, right that moment. You lean against the wall of a nearby building, thinking to yourself, "How could I have been so stupid! The Jewish God is not only a distant and powerful judge, but God can also be a friend, near to us, helping us when we feel sad or weak. After all, don't our prayers call God *Shechinah, Avinu,* and *Hamakom,* all names which are intimate and close? Of course! Right under my nose was the answer: I can find the God I need completely within Judaism."

You say a prayer of thanks to God who made school children your teachers. They have guaranteed a Jewish future for you and for your family after you. With a joyful, beaming face, you stride away, elated and happy, glad to be Jewish and able to pray to a living and loving God.

END

92

The ship sails southward, up the Nile River. You crouch, hidden beneath a pile of bags filled with beans. For several days, you must remain concealed. Even though you paid the captain of the ship a large sum of money to get you away from Alexandria, you cannot know whether he will keep his bargain or turn you in to a Roman garrison.

Finally, you feel free to emerge from your hiding place, and you actually enjoy the rest of the journey to the military outpost of Elephantine. You are farther than ever from Jerusalem, but at least you are safe.

On a military expedition to the land of Ethiopia, you meet and fall in love with an Ethiopian. Your spouse will be black, but, after all, so was the Queen of Sheba who married King Solomon. Others of your group also find spouses, and you all agree that this is a favorable situation, provided the new husbands and wives will convert to Judaism, a step they gladly agree to take. With them, you settle and begin a new life in a new country.

You recall the words of the prophet Isaiah who predicted, "She'ar yashuv," a remnant of the people will return. You and your friends and your new families will be that remnant. You will keep Judaism alive in this Ethiopian wilderness. Someday in the future, perhaps long after you are dead, your children will be able to return to Zion. Meanwhile, far away from Roman oppression, you will preserve the holy faith. The idea of this mission of survival gladdens and excites you. Your life has great meaning, and you are happy with your fate.

END

93

You stowaway on a trading ship, the same kind on which you once traveled as a privileged and honored guest. Now, you must hide in a suffocating, stench-filled corner, as far below the deck as possible. A sailor you have bribed brings you a bit of water and food each day, but you remain miserable, cramped, hungry, and wet. It is only after two weeks that the ship docks at Antioch, and you are able to slip over the side and swim to the shore.

Antioch has become a center of the Christian faith. The bishop of the city is one of the most important men in the new religion, and thousands of converts to Christianity throng the streets. As a Jew, you feel uncomfortable among them and decide that you cannot remain in the city. Driven from Antioch by their presence, you are also pulled to return to *Eretz Yisrael* by a strong and irresistible force. You feel that you do not wish to live anywhere except in Zion. But you have also heard that the Romans in Palestine have offered a reward for the capture of any leader of the defeated revolt and that your name has even been mentioned. Perhaps it would be dangerous to return, and you had best find another place to live.

If you decide to return to Eretz Yisrael,
despite the danger, by traveling south toward
the Galilee,
turn to page 122.

If you choose to find a less dangerous place
to live,
turn to page 123.

94

Some people give you a single coin; others contribute leather bags full of money. You express the thanks of the community and the prayer that God will bless them for their generosity. However much each can donate, you accept it with a smile and gratitude.

Some coins, however, give you special pleasure to accept. After the destruction of Jerusalem, the Romans minted coins with the legend "Judaea Capta," Judea has been taken. They arranged that these coins be circulated throughout their empire so that everyone would learn about their victory and about what would happen to anyone who opposed Roman power. Of course, many such coins have found their way to Alexandria, a city where trade and commerce lead to the frequent exchange of money.

It is these coins you especially seek out. When one is contributed to the *tzedakah* collection, you put it aside in a separate bag. Others in the Jewish community wonder about this strange fascination. "Why are you doing this?" they ask. "What special purpose have you found for these coins?"

You smile broadly and explain. "These coins were struck to humiliate us, to advertise our defeat and the destruction of Jerusalem. Now, I collect them and send them with a special messenger to the Jewish community of Jerusalem. What was meant for our shame is now the source of support for those who would keep the *Shechinah* in the land of Zion. Is that not just and fair? I have found a way to turn history around, and it makes me very happy that our defeat now paves the way for our victory."

END

95

Every day, you walk through the city, stopping at large business offices and small stalls in the marketplace. Some people advise you only to collect *tzedakah* from the rich people, but you respond that everyone, even the poorest Jew, has a right to give charity. "A pile of small coins," you tell them, "still adds up to a lot of help for poor people."

As you pass across the public market one day, you hear two men discussing the *haftarah* that had been chanted in the synagogue last *Shabbat.* One of the men objects to the prophetic lesson. "Ezekiel says that only the sinner will die, that the righteous man will always live. I don't see that happening in real life. Good people seem to suffer, and bad people sometimes appear to be rewarded. God doesn't play fair."

His comments provoke your thought, and you wonder if he is right or wrong. First you were engaged in business; then you were occupied collecting for charity. You have never had the time to think of such deep questions. Perhaps the time has come to look into some of the issues raised in the discussion you overheard.

If you decide that caring for poor Jews is still
your first priority,
turn to page 112.

If you choose to spend your time answering
serious questions,
turn to page 113.

96

On *Shabbat,* they seek to tell the good news of the new faith. The natural place for them to preach this message is in the synagogue of the Jewish community of Rome. After all, if they have been saved from damnation because of their new beliefs, shouldn't they share that hope with others?

This kind of evangelism may be their goal, but it is certainly not what the members of the synagogue have in mind. When they begin to deliver their message, the worshipers take offense and become incensed. "How dare you come into this holy synagogue and tell us about a pretender, about an idol! Jesus was nothing but a man, like us, not a god. No one can be God but Adonai! Get out! Go away!"

The new Christians flee from the synagogue, dodging stones, with jeers and rejection ringing in their ears. They are hurt, both physically and emotionally. These are supposed to be their people, friends. They were doing a *mitzvah* by helping them find salvation. Yet the Jews have rejected this good news, and this makes the new Christians angry.

Now, they realize the truth. Converting the Jews represents an impossible dream. They are too stiff-necked to change their beliefs. They have rejected the Christ, and they have spurned all who speak for him. Those who follow Jesus can no longer consider themselves Jews. Irrevocably, they will be Christians. The break is complete and permanent. From now on, there will be two different religions.

END

97

The new Christians are convinced that they can attract a large following among the pagans of Greece and Rome if only they can connect the new faith with the practices of the "mystery religions." "We've got to do two things," they say. "First, we cannot continue with the strict observance of the laws in the Torah. No one will want to join a church that demands all that Judaism asks of its members. If Jesus came to fulfill the Hebrew prophecies, then the Law is no longer necessary. Let people be saved only by their faith in Jesus. Second, let us make our common meal more like the mystery meal of the pagans. When we eat the bread and drink the wine, let us believe that we are eating the body and the blood of our god, just as they do in their cults."

You cannot believe your ears. All these compromises; all these changes. Surely, this is not what Jesus, the Jew from Bethlehem, would have wanted. Maybe, you think to yourself, you have made a terrible mistake. Maybe even being around these people is wrong.

You think for a very long time about such serious matters. Hiding with the new Christians has helped you stay safe, and some of their beliefs and ideas are attractive. They're nice people, and you've thought many times about joining them. But, finally, you come to a conclusion. You must return to Judaism.

You climb out of the catacombs and begin the most important walk of your life as, step by step, you head for the synagogue.

Turn to page 65.

98

From Rome, they walk to the port of Ostia. You go with them, hoping to travel closer to Palestine and, one day, return home. From Ostia, you take a coastal trading ship on the Mediterranean Sea, around the boot of Italy and into the port of Corinth. The dock area of the city is busy with merchants buying and selling all sorts of wares. Overwhelmed by the noise, you quickly leave this commercial zone and make your way to the house where the Christian community of the city gathers. There, you are warmly greeted. They are glad to have other missionaries who will tell the story of Jesus.

Like the Apostles, the disciples of Jesus, your friends begin their mission among the less fortunate men and women of the city, the poor. If these poor people do find work at all, they earn very little money, and they live in terrible conditions. But the missionaries offer them hope, preaching that "the meek shall inherit the earth." Many of the people accept the new faith because they believe that faith in Jesus promises them a better future.

The message is not so well received on the docks. Workers there resent what the missionaries have to say. "If the poor will do better in the future," the dock workers say, "then that must mean that the poor will take our jobs away. We can't let that happen!"

The next time you accompany your friends when they are preaching their message in that part of the city, a riot breaks out. "Here's the messenger of the bad news," the angry workers shout, turning on you with vicious looks. The last thing you ever see is a shower of rocks descending on you.

END

99

Antioch is, perhaps, the most important city on the eastern Mediterranean. But you are unhappy there—it's not Palestine, the Holy Land. The Christians are also not content—Jesus never lived in Antioch, never set foot there, and they really want to be close to the holy places where the savior walked. Thus, you all leave Antioch and travel south to Capernaum at the northern end of the Sea of Galilee. You settle there, praying every Sabbath at the synagogue (now a church) where Jesus himself prayed. For different reasons, each of you can feel the holiness of the place, and it gives you great joy and strength.

As they preach the message of Jesus, they tell how he was a fisher of men, how he taught his disciples to cast a net of salvation and draw in men and women who would gain eternal life. The parable's image persuades many to join the church.

But another preacher also comes to this location, a *rabbi* who disputes that claim. He says that Christian words are a snare, a trap for innocent people, offering them nothing. The Christians claim to offer hope, but it is, in fact, deception.

With sadness, your friends turn away from the *rabbi*. The gulf between Christianity and Judaism has widened to a point where no one can bridge it. There can be no friendship, no sharing. Each of you must continue in your chosen way, each believing that your way is right. The bad feelings cause you grief. You wish it could be otherwise, but, at least for a while, it cannot. You walk away.

END

100

You enter the synagogue on the next *Shabbat* and take your accustomed seat. As you look around, you notice that many of the worshipers are not Jewish; that's not unusual. After the *Tefillah* and the reading of the Torah, the prayer leader turns to them and asks them to leave. It's that way every *Shabbat,* and no one is surprised.

Then, the leader opens the Bible and, after a blessing of praise for God, he begins to chant the prophetic reading, the *haftarah.* As it is only a few weeks before *Rosh Hashanah,* the selection is from Isaiah. This selection portrays a wonderful future for the Jewish people. All their dreams and hopes will soon come true, while their enemies will be devastated and destroyed.

The next day, you pause from your work and smile. A *haftarah* like that may be embarrassing if it is read in the presence of non-Jews; they may even dislike us, saying that we are exalting ourselves at their expense. That's certainly not a good way to make friends. That *haftarah* could not have been read before the dismissal of the non-Jews. You were right! Jews should be Jews, and everyone else should believe whatever they want.

You are happy and content. The decision to oppose conversion satisfies you, and you can hardly wait for the next *Shabbat* and its comforting prophetic reading.

E N D

101

As you enter the Forum, you meet an aristocratic Roman woman who has frequently been a customer of yours. She greets you and then asks, "I've been wondering. Why didn't your God destroy the sun, the moon, and the stars? Many people worship these heavenly bodies. Wouldn't it have been better if God had destroyed such competition?"

This challenge from such an aristocratic Roman woman intrigues you. You think quickly. You know that it is really a trick question, and your answer must be correct. "No, indeed! God would only destroy the heavenly lights if they were really gods. But they're not. Only God is God; the others have no power whatsoever. But, if God had destroyed them, then people might have thought they were, in fact, divine. To leave them as they were tells people that, without God, the sun, moon, and stars are nothing."

She applauds your answer. "Well done, my friend. Let us talk tomorrow about your God."

As you walk away from her, you realize why Eleazar ben Azariah was right. This intelligent woman would be a good Jew; to bring people like her into the Jewish community would strengthen the people and enrich the faith. You become active in spreading the teachings of Judaism among non-Jews. Sharing the joys of being Jewish becomes your passion, and you are satisfied that you have made the right choices.

END

102

As you enter the synagogue, you notice a stranger sitting at one of the desks. He has a Hebrew book in front of him, but he is not reading. You approach him and ask, "May I help you?"

"Yes, indeed," he responds. "I am not Jewish, but I would like to learn about your faith. Unfortunately, I do not read Hebrew, so all of your writings are a mystery to me. Can you teach me?"

You look down at the book he has in front of him, at his finger pointing to some words on an open page. You cannot believe your eyes; it is as though God had sent you a sign.

"Do you see these words?" you ask him. "They say 've'ahavta lere'acha kamocha,' love your neighbor as yourself. It's one of the most important teachings of Judaism. In fact, Akiba, our greatest sage, said that everything else in Judaism was a commentary on this Torah verse. Of course, I shall try to teach you."

As you continue his instruction, you realize the joy that comes from bringing new knowledge to another person. Teaching makes you happy, and you commit the rest of your life to helping other people learn. "After all," you remind yourself, "did not our teachers say that the study of Torah is more important than anything else?" You certainly think it is.

END

103

Rabbi Meir is convinced that a terrible danger confronts Jews. "It is not the Roman army of which I am afraid," he explains. "In this time of confusion and chaos, we may lose sight of what it means to be a Jew; we might forget how to practice our religion. Somehow, we must collect all our wisdom together. Otherwise, we shall split into many different kinds of Judaism and even become separate religions. God did not reveal the Torah to us for us to lose it now."

He is right. You join his academy where many young scholars are collecting the various traditions within Judaism and writing them down. If there were only one book with everything in it that a Jew should do, then it could be copied and sent everywhere in the Jewish world. Then, all Jews would be able to be faithful to true Jewish practice.

Because of your experience in Rome, you are assigned to work on the chapter called "Avodah Zarah," Foreign Worship. The work is hard, and you spend long days at your desk. You know that you will never be able to finish the task, but you are content to add your part. Someone else will follow you and, perhaps, someday, it will be completed. Meanwhile, you realize that you are doing very important work. That understanding gives meaning and purpose to your life.

END

104

Rabbi Akiba turns to you and asks, "Can all the Jews of Rome really understand the Hebrew words of the Torah?"

You think for a moment, then reply, "Not really. Some of the older ones still remember the holy tongue, but the children speak Latin and sometimes Greek." Suddenly, you understand the wisdom of his question. A new translation of the Bible into Latin has been circulated throughout the Mediterranean world. Although there is an accurate Greek translation called the Septuagint, this new translation includes many mistakes. "You are right, honored Rabbi. We could really use a new translation so that these errors would be replaced by the truth."

Akiba takes your advice. A convert named Aquila of Pontus is hired to prepare a new Greek version of the Torah. Every day, as you pass the academy where he is working, you peek through the window. Although you are no scholar, you recognize the important contribution you have made. The correct understanding of the Torah will be preserved because you have convinced Rabbi Akiba to sponsor this new work, which comes to be known as the "Targum," the Aramaic word for "translation." That you have been able to make such a contribution to the survival of Judaism's most precious and holy book gives you great joy and satisfaction.

END

105

Residents of the Galilee help you hide from the Romans. In caves, in barns, in houses, in almost every place, moving daily to avoid capture, you continue to teach Torah. Several times, Roman soldiers nearly come upon you. You are extremely frightened because you know that they will torture and eventually kill you if they catch you.

Although the thought of capture terrifies you, you recognize that times of trouble call for extraordinary measures. "It's particularly in such days," Gamaliel tells you, "that your work is most important. If Hadrian can stop us from teaching Torah and reorganizing Jewish life, we shall perish. The only way to keep Judaism alive is to disobey Rome and honor our covenant with God."

As you teach and study, you keep detailed notes of what you learn. You realize that someday they may be useful to another scholar. It is as though you were planting an olive tree that would take many years to bear fruit. While the fruit may benefit only your children or grandchildren, you tell your students that you are planting for the Jewish future.

E N D

106

Reluctantly, you accept the truth. The Romans have made it so difficult to teach Judaism in the Galilee that you must turn toward the east and find another place to continue your studying and instruction.

Rabbi Nathan tells you of a far-off Jewish community, nestled between the valleys of the Tigris and Euphrates Rivers, where friendly rulers have encouraged the growth of Jewish academies. "Let us go to Pumbedita," he suggests. "There we shall be welcome, and we shall be able to do what we believe God wants us to do. It will be better to study the Torah outside of Israel than to live here without the Torah."

You agree, and the two of you set off on an eight hundred-mile journey through mountains, deserts, and down the famous river valleys of Mesopotamia until you finally reach Pumbedita. There the Jewish community welcomes you and agrees to support you while you study and teach.

Nathan is a much better scholar than you are, and soon his opinions are quoted widely throughout the Jewish world. He becomes known as Nathan Ha-Bavli, Nathan the Babylonian, while you remain a simple, unknown student. But you know that you are doing important work, keeping a record of his ideas and interpretations of the Torah. "You may seem less important than I am," he tells you, "but my words would be lost without you."

You both laugh. You're a team, and you are both helping keep Judaism alive for future generations.

END

107

Roman soldiers burst into the room and capture everyone. Your students are chained together and dragged off. They will probably be sold as slaves to work on Roman ships or in the homes of rich Roman landowners.

You are tied up and led to the main gate of the town, the place where judges used to sit and explain the Torah to the people. Now, however, that is forbidden. The soldiers tie you to a post and tease you: "See if you can teach the cursed Torah to the people now, Rabbi!"

The Roman soldiers stack a pile of wood around your feet and cover your body with wet rags. When the smoke from the fire they have built begins to rise, the rags will cause the fire to burn you more slowly so that your death will be even more agonizing. *"Shema Yisrael,"* you cough out, the smoke filling your nose and throat, "Hear, O Israel: the Lord is our God, the Lord is One."

Suddenly, a Roman soldier dashes up to you and rips the rags from your body. The flames rush up with fierce heat, and you want to scream. Instead, you twist your head toward the soldier and, with your last breath, say, "Thank you. You, too, will have a place in the world to come."

END

108

Fearfully, you open the door, only to find one of the members of the town council. He is jumping up and down with happiness. "The emperor is dead. Hadrian has been assassinated. The new emperor has cancelled his hated decrees, and we may now study Torah and act in public as Jews again. Long live the new emperor!"

You can hardly believe your ears. Years of persecution and hiding are over; you have won. Rather, you should say that God has triumphed over the evil idolators of Rome. Perhaps Hadrian's death is really part of God's plan. Together with other students, you offer a prayer of thanksgiving to the God who cared for the patriarchs and matriarchs and who now cares for you all.

The next day, you think to yourself: "We came very close to losing. We carried lots of Jewish knowledge in our heads. What if we had been killed? That wisdom would have been lost. We cannot allow that to happen. Judaism is too important to lock it up in the memory of mortal human beings. We must write down what we know so that it will be preserved for future generations."

Knowing that you are right, you bid farewell to your friends and students and leave for the academy of Rabbi Yehuda Ha-Nasi in Bet Shean. There you will be able to accomplish your goal of writing down the ideas and practices by which a Jewish person should live.

Turn to page 39.

109

When the *Shabbat* concludes, you and your friends agree: "We should do this every *Shabbat* evening. The prayers we say will be just like the sacrifices of the priests. It was so wonderful, so beautiful, so holy in that room. We have made our dining table into a replacement for the altar of the Temple."

Still, you miss the Temple. A trip to Jerusalem, however, cures you of this feeling. When you visit the holy site, all you see is a pile of rubble and burned up debris. Already, people are building houses on top of what once were the stones of God's holy house. Now, all you can see are tiny corners of stone, peeking up from under the dirt, and a thick layer of ashes and charred wood. Now you fully realize that the Temple is gone, never to be rebuilt in your lifetime—perhaps not for a very long time.

You return to Tiberias and reenter your little synagogue. For many generations, you decide, this simple room will be the center of the Jewish people. The synagogue will have to serve as the sanctuary of Israel. There is no choice. You and your friends turn all your attention to creating a service which will be dramatic and meaningful for the people. "That's the only way we're ever going to survive," you all agree. And so, with a prayer to God for help in your new endeavor, you turn to the task of saving the Jewish people.

END

110

As you return to B'nai B'rak, you see a large and noisy crowd in the public square. Quickly, you run to join them, asking what has happened. "It's the emperor Hadrian. In Rome, he has issued orders. We are no longer allowed to study the Torah. We can no more circumcise our sons. We cannot even ordain *rabbis.* If this is allowed to continue, it means the end of Judaism!"

Akiba ben Yosef, Eliezer ben Hyrcanus, and other community leaders are getting ready to travel to Rome. They will appeal to Hadrian to change his mind. When you ask to go with them, they agree.

After more than three weeks on a sailing ship and a walking trip from Ostia to Rome, your party is accorded an audience with the emperor. Akiba speaks eloquently for the delegation, but it doesn't seem to matter. Hadrian responds with contempt. "You, Jews, want special favors, but you will do exactly what I say. The empire cannot tolerate a group such as you which holds itself superior to everyone else. Now, get out!" And, with that, he waves you away with a sharp and final motion of his hand.

You return to *Eretz Yisrael* dejected, wondering how Judaism and Jews will ever survive. Akiba has been very quiet during the entire trip. He spent most of the time sitting, thinking by the rail of the ship. As you disembark at Ptolemais, he calls you and whispers, "I have a plan."

Turn to page 121.

111

Ishmael, it turns out, is a much gentler person than Akiba. While the latter is ready to go to war against Rome, Ishmael prefers a more peaceful approach. "Torah will be preserved and so will Judaism," he tells his students, "if we study and pray and, especially, if we write down as much as possible. That way, it can be passed on to future generations."

With his students, Ishmael undertakes a project. All of you copy down as many of the interpretations of the books of Exodus, Leviticus, and Numbers as you can remember. Sometimes, you write "midrashim," legends, that even contradict others. "No matter," Ishmael counsels you. "I don't know which is the right idea and which is the wrong one. Let us save all the possible interpretations. Some time in the future, scholars who are wiser than we will make the decision. Meanwhile, it is our task to save the tradition of Judaism from destruction."

You share that task. It is not easy. Your fingers ache with cramps at the end of the day, and your eyes are bleary with fatigue from copying legends, stories, and ideas about the Bible for eight or nine hours. Still, you are not unhappy because you have been chosen to fulfill a great *mitzvah:* to keep the faith of Judaism and the people of Israel alive for future generations.

END

112

You remember reading in the Bible how another Jew, long ago, had tried to solve the mystery of reward for good people and punishment for the bad—and how it doesn't always seem to work out right. Job wanted to know, and God spoke to him. Out of a whirlwind, Job was told that people will never understand all the ways God works, that all they can do is have faith and trust God.

If Job couldn't figure out the answer, you doubt that you could either. You're sure it is better for you to continue doing *mitzvot* and tending to those matters you can actually influence. You do, however, change one thing. As you continue your rounds, collecting money for the poor, you begin to give short talks. "God," you say, "is a great mystery. But we must trust; we must have faith. If life does not seem fair to us now, know that, after we die, God will straighten everything out. The good that you do today will not be forgotten; your reward is sure to come. Therefore, be generous with the unfortunate and fill my *tzedakah* cup."

As you grow old, you are praised for your wisdom and your devotion to the cause of the needy. You are known as one who took care of God's children, and this is all the recognition you need.

END

113

You turn quickly to the doubting man and say, "How can you possibly challenge God? What are you, some kind of genius, that you know better than the Almighty what is right and wrong? Remember what we sing at the *Pesach seder,* 'Dayenu,' it would have been enough. Don't you remember all the ways God has taken care of the Jewish people during the past, how we were saved from Egyptian slavery, how we received the Torah, how we were fed manna and quail in the wilderness, how water spurted forth from a rock—don't you remember? And don't you think that God will continue to take care of us today and tomorrow?

"In our prayers, we call God *'Avinu* sheh bashamayim,' our Father in heaven. Do you know what that means? God is concerned about us, as a parent looks after children. We may not be able to answer all the tricky questions of the world, but we know that God will never abandon the Jewish people. Why, in the Torah, we were called "am segulah," a specially treasured people, and, if it says that in the Torah, you can certainly trust it."

You can hardly believe that you gave such a sermon, a long talk without any preparation. You turn to go and discover that many people had gathered around to listen to your words. Now, they clap their approval. Perhaps you have a third career in your future, teacher and preacher. It wouldn't be such a bad way to grow old. You'll have to think about the possibility.

END

114

For the rest of your life, you travel through the Mediterranean region, stopping first at one Jewish community, then another. Each time you arrive, you go to the synagogue and speak with the assembled congregation. "It is a great *mitzvah*," you remind them, "to support those Jews who have remained in the Holy Land. Each of you is required to contribute the equivalent of one-half shekel to help those Jews maintain Jewish life in the land of Israel. You should consider such a contribution to be a great privilege." And almost everyone comes forward to deposit this small amount in your charity bag.

When you return to *Eretz Yisrael,* a sense of joy and satisfaction overwhelms you. Even the air seems to make you feel wiser, stronger, and holier. You visit the city of Jerusalem to pray as close to the remains of the holy Temple as you can. Only a small part of the outside wall, west of the piles of rubble and debris of the Temple itself, still stands, but you are sure that this sacred building will one day be reconstructed.

Meanwhile, you are very sure that you are doing exactly what God wants you to do, and that knowledge makes your life worthwhile. You are a happy and contented person.

E N D

115

Day by day, you crisscross the region of Yavneh, just as others do near their hometowns. When you come to a vineyard, you ask the owner to contribute some grapes so that the poor can have wine for Passover. You go to the owner of the winepress and secure his promise to turn those grapes into wine. The baker is asked to contribute *matzot,* as the farmer was urged to give some wheat for the miller to make into flour. Everyone in the community donates a little so that the responsibility for making sure that the poor can observe Passover properly is shared by everyone. That way, everyone contributes something, and no one is asked to do too much.

You also arrange a system by which the poor can come to a window, where you cannot see their faces, and receive *Pesach* provisions. Thus no one will be embarrassed to ask for help.

The *rabbis* of the *Bet Din* approve of your system and write it down so that other cities can follow the same procedure. "You have done well, my friend," the head of the rabbinical court says to you. "You have made it possible for everyone to observe our religion without problems. God is surely smiling down upon you."

END

116

In a long file, you walk the several miles from Yavneh to the coast of the Mediterranean Sea. When you arrive on the beach, you tell the students to sit down, take off their sandals, and put their coats in a neat pile. The students become excited when you bring out a picnic lunch. Everyone says the *Motzi* together, thanking God for the bread, and then they eat. One student, who has a habit of whining and complaining, runs up to you. "Rabbi, please tell the others to stop. They are kicking up the beach, and I have to eat the sand which is there." You tell him not to complain and simply to move from one place to another.

After lunch, you make everyone wade into the water. "Students," you say, "Judaism is so much more than praying and studying. Judaism covers our entire lives. If you do not know how to take care of your bodies properly, you cannot fulfill the Jewish religion completely. Today, we are going to learn to swim."

You and the students spend the rest of the afternoon at the beach. With a lot of coughing and swallowed water, and a lot of laughter, too, most of you manage to learn to swim, at least to float. Trekking back to Yavneh, you smile. What a wonderful life it is to work with young people and see them develop into fine adults! You are a happy person.

END

117

As you sit in the synagogue on *Shabbat* morning, you listen to the *haftarah* from the prophet Jeremiah. He speaks in glowing terms of the Rechabites, an ancient group of desert dwellers who were righteous and pure. The message of Jeremiah is clear. Things were better before people moved to cities; in crowded conditions, people turn to bad behavior. You reach the conclusion that God must certainly favor agriculture and rural life. After all, so much of the Jewish religion is based on farming and raising animals; most of the festivals are agricultural.

If this is what God likes, this is what you will do. You turn to a rich landowner, Tarfon, who is also a *rabbi*. He willingly arranges that a part of his land be turned over to your school so that you can teach the students farming and shepherding skills on it. Some students specialize in raising figs and apples; others plant vines and collect the grapes for wine. There are fields for barley, onions, garlic, and corn. Other students take care of goats, chickens, and oxen. Your favorite activity, however, is planting a small grove of olive trees. You know that they will not bear any fruit for a long time, in fact, until after you are dead. "But," you tell the students, "we must always look to the future. I am planting these trees for my children and grandchildren. I have hope for tomorrow."

END

118

You have noticed that, with the Romans in control of the entire area from southern Anatolia to Egypt, more travelers appear on the roads. In your talks with the members of the city council about your new school, you propose to train students to care for the needs of these wayfarers. You call your plan the "M and M Solution." They agree to let you undertake this idea.

The first "M" stands for "mansiones," the Latin word for "inns." Because anybody traveling will certainly need a place to eat and sleep, you will teach some of the students how to cook, how to serve meals, how to run a wayside inn. They will provide for the care of the men and women who travel the roads near Yavneh. The second "M" represents "mutationes," the Latin word for "changing stations." Because the travelers will need fresh horses when they leave your inns, some of the students will be trained to take care of animals. With the new mansiones and mutationes, your students will be able to support themselves and even contribute to the community's *tzedakah* collection.

Everyone approves of the "M and M Solution." Even the Roman governor comes to the opening of the first establishment. As your students go out into the world, you are happy. You may have saved only a few individuals from poverty, but you feel as though you have saved the entire world.

END

119

As you travel north with Yose ben Halafta, you notice a very strange odor about him. In fact, you think to yourself that he stinks. Very privately, you ask another teacher about this. He explains, "Yose is, by profession, a tanner who works with animal skins and liquids that smell bad. It is a very humble occupation, but he is proud that he does not have to take money from the Jewish community. Forget the smell; listen to what he has to teach for he is a genius."

You take that good advice and concentrate on Yose's wisdom. He has some extremely strong views about the school you are about to establish. "We must concentrate," he demands, "on two things: the history of our people—after all, did not the Torah teach that we shall tell the events of the past to our children—and the very finest students. We do not have the time to teach ignoramuses. Let the *am ha'aretz,* the unlearned person, go to learn somewhere else. We only want the best young people!"

Such a group of outstanding young students gathers, and you and the other teachers begin to work with them. As you come to know them, you realize that they are, indeed, the future security of the Jewish people. They are truly gifted students. Teaching them is a joy, and you understand that your contribution through them to the future of Jewish life will be considerable.

END

120

Eleazar ben Azariah's academy is different from the others. He welcomes any student who wants to learn, regardless of whether the student is brilliant or stupid. "Perhaps they will learn a lot, perhaps only a little. Who knows? But who are we to say that they should not have the chance to learn something?"

You agree with him. Among his teachings is one which you post on the wall of your classroom: "There can be no right conduct without Torah."

One day, Eleazar enters your room during a lesson and commands you to stop teaching. You are accustomed to this kind of behavior from him. He sometimes acts like a king, but he always means well and you don't get upset. "Go and pack your bags," he orders. "We are going to Rome."

Your journey with Eleazar takes several weeks, but finally you arrive in the capital of the Roman Empire. There, you receive an audience with the emperor who gives Eleazar permission to establish schools in many cities. Eleazar has told you that he is worried. Many Gentiles have converted to Judaism, and it will be necessary to continue teaching them. The new schools will welcome those who have chosen to become Jewish and help them learn enough to act as good Jews. Eleazar ben Azariah then turns to you. "You," he orders, "are to be the head of the school here in Rome." And so you spend the rest of your life contentedly, teaching the Torah in a foreign land to people who have chosen to join you and God's holy people.

E N D

121

You have never seen Akiba so angry. All the emotion that has been stored up during the trip back from Rome now breaks forth in flashing, dark eyes and a voice full of fury. "No Roman emperor is going to stop us from following the will of the God who spoke to Moses at Sinai. Never! We shall continue to be Jews long after Hadrian is dead, long after Rome loses its empire and becomes a wasteland, inhabited only by wild animals. We shall prevail."

Eliezer interrupts. He stomps back and forth and then throws open his robe. You never thought you would see something like this. On his belt is a dagger, long and curved, sharp and shining. "Weapons," he growls, "are an adornment for a man. We must resist the Romans even if it means taking up arms and killing them. Before the Torah, everything must give way!"

Akiba now continues. "There is one man I know who can lead us. Some say that his name is Shimon bar Koz'ba, but I am convinced that it is bar Kochba, 'son of the star.' This man is the messiah. He will direct our armies; he will restore Jewish government to *Eretz Yisrael;* he will bring us to a future time of glory and brightness. We shall follow him to victory."

With Akiba's ringing words in your ears, you join the forces of Shimon bar Koziba (Kochba).

Turn to page 41.

122

The walk from Antioch to the northern Galilee covers a distance of about 150 miles. You keep to the flat plains along the seacoast, making the journey an easy ten-day adventure. Each night, you find a quiet place on the beach, pull your cloak over you, and place a rounded stone under your head as a pillow as Jacob did in the biblical Book of Genesis.

One night, just north of Sidon, you lie relaxed, the lapping waters of the Mediterranean having lulled you into a peaceful and serene half-sleep. While you slumber, you have a dream. Or, is it a vision? It seems so real. A voice speaks to you, and you are aware of a sharp and blinding light. You wrestle your eyes open, but the light is so strong that you cannot see; you only hear.

The voice tells you that you have been chosen for the special mission of bringing hope to those who have remained in *Eretz Yisrael.* "But how shall I do this?" you respond. Suddenly, the answer is clear. You have always been a talented artist; now you will put your gifts to use by creating images of hope. People will see them; they will pray for the coming of the Messiah, for the return of Jewish rule to the Holy Land. You have been selected to place the vision of a better future before their eyes.

You awaken. Could you have heard the voice of God? You'll never really know, but the message remains clear and persuasive. You complete your journey and spend the rest of your days in a town in the Galilee, designing and making the mosaic floor of a small synagogue. The shofar of redemption symbolizes the hope you want to bring to the people. Your life is fulfilled and happy.

E N D

123

You board a ship at Antioch and sail southward to the port city of Joppa. When the ship ties up at the dock in this small, shallow harbor, you see piles of merchandise: Egyptian cotton and linen, donkeys and camels for sale or hire, jugs of wine and olive oil—everything anyone could want to purchase. People dash back and forth, buying and selling, shouting, arguing. Food vendors push through the crowd, urging you to spend what few coins you have on their delicacies.

You discover another presence as well. Roman centurions and their soldiers elbow their way through the throng, pushing people to the ground, treating those in their way with extreme roughness. A merchant turns to you and says in a whisper, "If you think it's bad here, you should see what happens in Jerusalem!"

Almost immediately, you understand that you cannot remain in a country where such cruelty by foreign soldiers exists. You hear people talking of a Jewish community in Mesopotamia, left there from the days of the Babylonian Exile. They live beyond the borders of the Roman Empire, and you decide to travel to the valleys of the Tigris and Euphrates Rivers, to the city of Sura.

The caravan takes weeks and weeks to make the circuit of the "Fertile Crescent." Finally, you reach Sura and settle into a new life. Your skills as a scribe are needed in the academy, and you spend the rest of your days recording the learned discussions of Jewish law. In a small, but important, way you are working to preserve Judaism, making your future very pleasant.

END

124

Rabbi Yehuda assembles all the scholars of his academy and assigns each one a subject. One is asked to collect all the answers to questions about Jewish holy days. Another is told to find responses to questions about laws dealing with business. Still a third will research the areas of criminal behavior, and so forth. Each scholar and a group of students will write out the answers in a systematic and clear fashion so that anyone who has a question about how to act as a Jew can find the answer easily and quickly.

As the process reaches completion, Rabbi Yehuda collects all the writings into one book which he calls the "Mishnah," a set of teachings about the Torah. "Here it is," he announces. "Everything a Jew might want to ask about the Torah is answered right here in the "Mishnah." Scribes can copy it and carry it throughout the Jewish world. That way, all Jews will be able to practice Judaism in the same way wherever they live. Well, my young friend, what do you think?"

"It's wonderful! But, you see, Rabbi Yehuda, I have a question. . . ."

E N D

Glossary

Am Ha'aretz · Literally, "people of the land." The term came to mean an ignoramus or unlearned person.

Avinu · Literally, "our father." A term used to refer to God.

Bet Din · A rabbinical court.

Diaspora · A Greek word meaning "dispersion" or "scattering." The term refers to Jews living outside *Eretz Yisrael*.

Eretz Yisrael · The land of Israel.

Etrog (Plural: Etrogim) · A citron. One of the four species of vegetation used to celebrate *Sukot* (see Leviticus 23:40).

Galut · The Hebrew word for "exile."

Haftarah · A selection from the biblical books of the Prophets read every *Shabbat* and holy day in the synagogue.

Hamakom · Literally, "the place." A term used to refer to God, meaning "the One who is every place" or "omnipresent."

Ketubah · A marriage contract.

Kiddush Hashem · Literally, the Hebrew for "sanctification of God's name." A worthy action by a Jew enhances the prestige of Judaism and adds to the glory of God. The original meaning signified martyrdom, the supreme sanctification of God.

Kuppah · Communal fund for the support of the poor.

Mashiach · Bible: someone anointed with holy oil and consecrated to a special purpose or mission by God. Post-biblical: Messiah who will restore Israel under a Davidic king and usher in an era of universal peace, plenty, and spiritual regeneration.

Matzah (Plural: Matzot) · Unleavened bread eaten during *Pesach,* symbolizing the hasty departure from Egypt. It reminds Jews of the need to help those today who must still eat the bread of affliction.

Mikveh · The ritual bath used for purification.

Mitzvah (Plural: Mitzvot) · Literally, the Hebrew word for "God's commandment." The word is usually used to mean a "good deed."

Motzi · The prayer recited before meals; grace.

Parnas (Plural: Parnasim) · The non-rabbinic leader or president of a congregation or community.

Pesach · The Festival of Passover, usually in April, during which Jews recall the Exodus from Egypt and pledge to help people everywhere become free.

Pithom and Raamses · The storehouse cities built for Pharaoh by Israelite slaves (see Exodus 1:11).

Rabbi · Literally, the Hebrew word for "my master" or "my teacher." The term refers to a Jew qualified to teach Jewish law.

Rosh Hashanah · Jewish New Year (see Leviticus 23:24 and Numbers 29:1).

Seder · Literally, the Hebrew word for "order." The word is used for the home or community Passover service which includes a ceremonial meal and the retelling of the story of the Exodus from Egypt.

Sela (Plural: Sela'im) · An ancient coin equivalent to two shekels.

Shabbat · The Sabbath.

Shaliach · A messenger from *Eretz Yisrael.*

Shavuot · The Festival of Weeks or Pentecost which commemorates both the spring harvest and the time of the giving of the Torah on Mount Sinai (see Exodus 23:16 and Numbers 28:26).

Shechinah · A term referring to God, meaning "the close or nearby presence of God."

Shema Yisrael · "Hear, O Israel. . . ." The title and first words of Judaism's most important prayer (see Deuteronomy 6:4–9).

Sukot · The Festival of Booths or Tabernacles which usually occurs in October. It recalls both God's goodness through the fall harvest and the Exodus from Egypt (see Exodus 23:16 and Leviticus 23:42–43).

Tamchui · Collection of food distributed daily from the Jewish communal kitchen for the poor.

Tefillah · The Hebrew word for "prayer." Technically, the word is applied to the central prayer of the Jewish worship service, composed of nineteen paragraphs on weekdays and seven on *Shabbat* and containing praise, thanks, and petitions of God. It is also known as the Amidah or Shemoneh Esreh.

Teyku · Aramaic for "Let it stand." Used at the end of an argument when no definite answer seems possible. It is also an abbreviation for the phrase, "Elijah the Tishebite will solve all difficulties."

Tzedakah · Charity or righteousness.

Printed in the United States
20994LVS00007B/106-306